Black Velvet
A Curvy Girl Musician Romance
Nichole Rose

Nichole Rose

Contents

Dedication

To you. You are brave enough, strong enough, good enough. You are enough.

About the Book

Every musician needs a muse...

Clayton

Addison Kissinger blew my mind the first time I met her.

Those sweet little lips whispering my name made me crazy.

She hasn't spoken to me since.

That hasn't stopped me from watching her.

Or kept me from craving her.

Half the world is screaming my name.

I want her begging it.

She's soft. Sweet. Sexy. *Mine.*

She doesn't know it yet, but she's about to find out.

Addison

I've loved Clayton Devine since the first time I set eyes on him.

So has the rest of the world.

He's a massive country music superstar.

Those skilled hands and that little boy smirk drive women wild.

I promised my best friend I would speak to him.

My boss just sent me on the road with him.

He probably thinks I'm just another annoying little fangirl.

He doesn't know it yet, but he's about to find out different.

Because I plan to bring this superstar to his knees.

Warning

When this older musician and his dream girl are thrown together, sparks hotter than a five-alarm fire will fly. If you enjoy obsessed musicians, heartfelt heroines, and karaoke hookups, you'll love Clayton and Addison. This sweet, steamy romance from Nichole Rose comes complete with a sticky-sweet and guaranteed HEA.

Chapter One

Addison

"Two lane blacktop in my rearview, don't know where I'm going next," I sing along to the radio, drumming my fingers against the steering wheel. I was supposed to be at work an hour ago, but there was an accident, so traffic has been at a standstill for the last two hours. The flames from the wreckage shot into the sky, roaring like they were alive. I'm half a mile away, and I could hear them.

The fire seems to be under control now, but thick black smoke still boils upward, covering the Nashville skyline in a dense, inky haze. Even with my windows up, I can smell it in the air, choking the city like smog.

The driver behind me lays on his horn for the tenth time in the last few minutes. I glance in my rearview to see him ranting like a lunatic with his head hanging out the window of his white Mercedes.

I swear, some people have no decency.

Someone may be seriously hurt or dead, but he's mad because he's in traffic.

I don't understand why people think that way, always putting themselves first and never considering anyone else. My best friend, Laney Briggs, says that's because my heart is bigger than the rest of my body. Maybe she's right. It just makes me sad that people get so caught up in their own little worlds that they never stop to think about anyone else.

Take *Two Lane Blacktop*, the song on the radio, for instance. It's full of so much raw emotion and yearning, yet no one ever asks Clayton Devine, the man who wrote it, why. They never ask why he's ashamed of himself or who he thinks he let down. They just ask what he's doing next...what he's releasing, where he's playing, if he's dating. It's ridiculous.

His entire album is genius. It's been sitting at the top of the charts in every major market since it released two months ago, but no one ever asks him what inspired it or why he wrote it. Everyone is more interested in what he can do for them than they are in him as a person.

It makes me sad. And not just because I've been in love with him since I started interning with his manager, Riley Jamison, last August. Clayton Devine is one of the greatest voices to come out of Nashville in the last half-century. As soon as he opens his mouth, pure gold spills out.

Traffic inches forward a few feet before coming to a stop again.

The guy behind me blows his horn and starts yelling out the window again.

"Jeez," I mutter, shaking my head. I turn up the radio, trying to drown him out. Listening to Clayton beats listening to him scream any day.

Riley discovered Clayton singing in his bar in Little Rock, Arkansas a few years ago. She and her husband, Cash, stopped to eat while Clayton was messing around on his guitar in the back. As soon as Riley heard him, she offered to represent him. The rest is pretty much history. His first album shot up the charts. His second did too. Now, he's considered one of the biggest names in country music, right alongside Kasen Alexander and Bentley Reynolds.

Women go crazy over him, which always seems to surprise him a little bit. I don't think he realizes just how gorgeous he is. But he is so darn sexy. He's built like a tree, tall, broad, unbending. He looks like a hot lumberjack...if lumberjacks dressed in all black and carried a guitar instead of an axe. Vivid tattoos run up and down his arms, offering little glimpses into the private life he guards so fiercely.

His dark hair is cut short on the sides but is a little wild on top. I always want to comb my fingers through it, just to see if it's as soft as it looks. He usually hides his forest green eyes behind a pair of dark sunglasses, but those eyes are intense. Brooding. Even his beard and mustache are sexy.

The first time I met him, I thought I was going to pass out. I managed to whisper hello, and then I forgot to release his hand. I think I held it for like five minutes before Riley asked me if I was going to let him go. She didn't mean to embarrass me, but I was mortified.

Clayton probably thought I was crazy!

I avoid him now. It's easier than humiliating myself in front of him again, and there's no telling what I'll do next. Talking to people makes me nervous on a good day. Talking to Clayton scares the crap out of me. I'm so afraid I'll reveal how much I love him. I know I don't stand a chance with him, but I still want to be able to talk to him, even if it's just to thank him for always being nice to me.

And he is so darn sweet to me. Even though I'm a complete spazz, he doesn't treat me that way. A lot of the other artists who come in are rude and demanding. They look right through me because I'm not important enough to notice. Not Clayton though. He always says hi to me and remembers my name. If he brings Riley coffee, he brings me coffee. He doesn't ever say anything about it, either. He just sits it on my desk, says my name, and then goes to see Riley.

I'm not certain, but I think he's the one who sent me flowers for my birthday a few months ago. The arrangement was massive and incredibly beautiful. The card said, 'Happy birthday, little one', but didn't say who it was from. It had to have cost him a fortune. Though, I guess when you make as much money as he does, dropping a few hundred dollars on flowers isn't a big deal.

My phone rings, startling me. I glance at the touchscreen and smile. It's Laney.

"I miss you!" I cry as soon as I answer. "Are you having fun?"

"Do you know what it's like having twenty-two annoying older brothers?"

"Um, no. I know what it's like having one adorable younger one."

"I'm surrounded by madmen and lunatics," she huffs, making me laugh. Laney just married Weston Davies, who plays hockey for the Nashville Predators. Since it's the middle of the season, they haven't really been able to go on a honeymoon, so she took a week off from the bookstore where she works parttime to travel to games with him.

She's had a huge crush on him since I met her our freshman year of high school. A couple months ago, she lost her dad to cancer. The last year has been really hard on her. It makes me happy to know she's happy. She deserves it. And it's obvious that Weston is crazy in love with her, which is adorable.

"You wanted to travel with the team," I remind her.

"That was before they adopted me," she says. "The attendant at the hotel smiled at me, so Theo and Gray ran and tattled to Wes that he was flirting with me. Wes dragged me off to have dirty hot sex in our room before the game. I think my vagina is broken."

I throw my head back and laugh. My best friend is kind of crazy. It's one of the reasons I love her so much. I never have to worry about being shy around Laney. She says more than enough for both of us. She's really sweet but she's also very outspoken.

"What are you doing?" she asks. "Are you at work?"

"Not yet. I'm stuck in traffic."

"Yuck."

"Clayton is supposed to be there today," I say, my voice soft. Butterflies dance in my belly. Sometimes, he looks at me and my entire body bursts into flames. I just want to clench my thighs together and whimper. Every other woman on the planet reacts the same way. There's just something deliciously sinful about him that makes you want to squirm.

When he's happy, he has the most wicked little boy smirk. Not even his beard hides it. He looks more like a rockstar than a country music artist, but he's so freaking beautiful. So is his voice. Lyrics drip from his full lips like velvet, brushing across my senses in a way that's downright criminal. I shiver every time he speaks in my general vicinity. I have to wear sweaters at work to hide my reaction to him.

I'm not doing a very good job hiding it. Cami Reynolds knows how I feel about him. I think my boss knows I have a massive crush on him too. She always watches me when I have to get anywhere close to him. She never says anything though. Riley is pretty much the best boss on the planet. She knows talking to people gives me anxiety, so she doesn't make me deal with people face to face often.

Instead, I help with photography and graphic design. I get to put together all the graphic elements used in social media campaigns for Saunders Management and the recording artists they represent. I also help out with portfolio photography. I spend my downtime weeding through demo tapes and searching out music on social media, looking for new and up-and-coming talent. I hope she hires me on at the end of my internship in May. I'm only a sophomore, but I'm working toward an integrated degree in art and music studies, my two great loves in life. Working for Riley would be a dream.

"Yes!" Laney crows into the phone. "It's about darn time. Are you going to talk to him today? You have to talk to him today. We had a deal."

"About that..."

"Nope. Nu-uh. No way, Addy," she says before I can even try to wiggle out of it. "A deal is a deal. I prostituted myself for charity, so now you have to say hello to Clayton."

"Just hello?" I ask, letting her get away with her revisionist history. She didn't prostitute herself. She spent fifty dollars to enter a Win a Valentine's Day Date with Weston contest. She won—he made sure of it—and now they're crazy happy together. And St. Jude Children's Research Hospital received a million-dollar donation.

"You can start there. Maybe throw in a 'how you doin' next," she says, dropping her voice low to imitate Joey from *Friends*.

"I'm going to throw up," I groan, anxiety churning in my stomach. When I was a little girl, I had a stutter. The words would get tangled up on my tongue and just wouldn't come out right. When I sang, I never stuttered, but if I talked, I did. Some of the girls in my class teased me about it a lot.

I went to a slumber party once, and they were teasing me, saying I was faking it since I could sing without stuttering. I ran off and ended up lost in the woods overnight. By the time a farmer found me the next morning, I was freezing and terrified. My dad is a popular entertainment lawyer with a lot of connections. The story was all over the news.

It took a lot of speech therapy to help me get over stuttering, but I finally managed to do it. I still get anxious around people though. It's the absolute worst around

Clayton. It's frustrating. There's a lot I want to say to him. I just can't seem to find my voice to say it.

"I'm a coward."

"You aren't," Laney says, her voice soft. She's one of the only people in the world who knows how I feel about Clayton or why I struggle to talk to people. "You can do this, Addy. You're so much braver than you think you are. Do you talk to Riley?"

"Yes."

"Cash?"

"Yes..."

"Kasen Alexander?"

"That's different," I protest. Riley and Cash, her husband, are so down-to-earth. And Kasen may be a big star, but he's also a lot like Laney. It's hard to stress and worry and freak about what I might say or how it might sound to him when he never knows what he's talking about or what's going to come out of his mouth. He's completely crazy! I also haven't been secretly in love with him for months.

"If Clayton is even half the man you tell me he is, there's nothing you could say that would make him treat you badly," Laney says.

She's right. Clayton would never make fun of me or be mean if I said something dumb.

"Besides, if you never speak to him, you'll always regret it," she says. "Don't let fear keep you from what might be the best decision you ever made."

"You're right," I say, letting off the brake to inch forward as traffic begins to creep along again.

"Of course I'm right," she says, laughing. "And you know how I know I'm right? Because when I let fear stand in my way not so long ago, my best friend told me to get my butt on a plane and go get my man. And I know for a fact that my best friend is a bad ass."

Oh, she's good at this.

"I'm going to do it," I say.

"Yeah?"

"I am. I'm going to talk to him today," I say.

"Dang right you are, sister!" Laney shouts into the phone, making me laugh again. God, I love her. I don't know what I would have done without her all these years. She never makes me feel guilty about my issues. She just jumps right in and says what I wish I could.

"Dinner when you get home?" I ask, hitting the brake as traffic stops again.

The angry man behind me lays on his horn, screaming obscenities out the window.

The guy in the F150 next to him must be as tired of hearing him as I am. He rolls his window down and shouts, "Shut the fuck up!".

"Yeah! Shut up already!" yells the driver of the Honda in front of me, sticking his head out the window.

"Oh my gosh!" I say, slapping a hand over my mouth to hide my laughter.

"Ah, traffic," Laney says, a smile in her voice. "I'll be home tomorrow night. Oh! You're on spring break all week! We can hang out while Weston is at practice."

"Sounds good to me." Since I'm an intern, I only work a few hours each day. Normally I would have class to fill the other hours, but with spring break, I'm all freed up.

"You better call me after you talk to Clayton."

"I will," I promise.

"Love you!"

"Love you too."

The car beeps when the call ends, and then Clayton's voice spills from the speakers again. I meld my voice to his and belt out the lyrics, feeling confident and excited...and a little bit terrified. I'm not going to let that stop me though. Not this time.

I'm talking to Clayton today, even if it kills me.

Chapter Two

Clayton

"What the fuck?" I growl, coming to a dead stop between the elevator doors. My eyes narrow on the empty desk where Addison Kissinger is supposed to be. I always schedule my meetings with Riley on days when Addison is scheduled to work, but her phone isn't clipped to her computer monitor and her heels aren't under her desk, which means she isn't here today.

She *always* kicks her shoes off when she's working. I think they pinch her adorable little toes, but I can't ask her that question, regardless of how many times I've worried about it. Addison don't say much. Actually, she don't speak to me at all. The first time I met her last August, she looked up at me through her long lashes, took my hand, and whispered hello in the sweetest voice I've ever heard...and that's the last time she spoke to me.

I've been going out of my mind ever since.

Addison is the kind of beautiful you expect to see tucked away in some fairytale castle, not working a desk in a talent management firm. Her jet-black hair is the sky, and those innocent cornflower blue eyes are the stars, shining like magic in the world. She's tiny and delicate, barely bigger than anything. But God, nothing has ever made my dick harder than she does when those pretty lips curve into a smile.

She's pure and innocent as an angel, completely oblivious to how enticing she is. But the way those hips move when she walks? *Damn.* Her tits are too big for that little bitty frame, but I spend a fair amount of my time dreaming about getting my mouth all over them anyway. She ever figures out just how beautiful she is, she's going to bring every man in her vicinity to their knees.

I'll put every single one of them down like rabid dogs.

Right or wrong, I want Addison Kissinger to be mine.

All it took was one look at her, and I was obsessed. Been that way every day since.

It's killing me that she's too afraid to speak to me. My little one is so shy and sweet. I've been trying to earn her trust, so she gives me that sweet voice again but I'm at my breaking point. I'm a desperate man, ready to do desperate things just to hear her say my name.

Ain't a man alive who wouldn't do the same if they knew her.

A lot of people in this town play the game. They're saccharine to your face, willing to blow smoke up your ass until it comes out your ears. As soon as you turn your back, the knives and claws come out. Addison isn't like that. She's genuinely, authentically, salt-of-the-earth *kind*. Caring. Compassionate. Sweet as the day is long.

She's also smart as all get out. The four-point-oh, full-ride, graduated early kind of smart. When she ain't busy, her nose is in a book. She loves classic literature and historical romance, especially Westerns. She may not talk to me, but I've shamelessly eavesdropped on enough conversations to know there's nothing about country music she don't know.

At nineteen, she's sixteen years younger than I am, but that don't seem to matter a whole hell of a lot. I accepted long ago that I'm a dirty old bastard for wanting her the way I do. I tried to fight it, tried to stop thinking about her. Wasn't any use. Some days, she's *all* I think about.

I should be ashamed of myself for the way I stalk her social media, just waiting for her to post something. Her posts are usually music related, snippets of lyrics she loves or stories about artists she admires. I think a few of those lyrics are original, but she never says so. Some of them are mine, which makes me feel like I'm bulletproof. She posts pictures with her best friend or her little brother sometimes, but most of her pictures are of places and things...and pets. I don't think she's ever met a dog or cat she didn't photograph.

The things I want to do to her would probably horrify her if she knew but I jack my cock every damn day, thinking about her pretty lips wrapped around it, or her on her back below me with my hand around her throat while she begs me to fuck her harder. Or her screaming the house down around me while I feast on her tiny pink asshole. I've fantasized about taking her every which way and loved every minute of it.

Which is all the proof I need that I don't deserve her. A man like me, one who has done the things I've done...I could never deserve an angel like her. My hands have spilled blood, touched all four walls of a prison cell. I've lied and stolen and been a thousand things I'd be ashamed to admit to a sweet little thing like her.

She's a shy young angel. I'm the old dirty bastard who thinks about tying her to my bed and fucking her until she breaks. I've tried to keep my distance. I've tried to avoid looking at her while I'm here. I started wearing sunglasses so she wouldn't see me staring at her. I don't want to frighten her. I just can't seem to keep my eyes off her.

My heart beat for the first time the day I met her.

It's beat *allegrissimo* for her every day since.

"Hey, Clayton," Cami Reynolds says, looking up from her desk when I finally step out from between the doors of the elevator so they stop trying to close on me. "Riley's waiting for you in her office."

"Thanks," I mutter and then hesitate for another long minute, trying to convince myself not to ask where Addison is at. It's not my business. I should mind my own, go see what Riley wants, and get out of here before I break.

"She's stuck in traffic," Cami says, her voice whisper quiet while I wrestle with my conscience. "She should be here soon."

I glance in her direction.

She gives me a knowing smile.

Shit. I guess my secret ain't so secret.

I jerk my chin in a nod and head toward Riley's office before she can ask me any of the questions I see brimming in her eyes. Cami is a sweet girl, one of a handful of people I actually don't mind being around. Don't particularly care to lose her friendship by confirming that I'm the creep who jerks off nightly to thoughts of her friend.

"Bentley, Cash, and Kasen are in there with her," she calls.

Well, hell.

Cami and Riley's husbands, and Kasen Alexander are decent, hard-working men who put their families ahead of all the bullshit that comes with money and fame. Down to the last one, they're madly in love with their wives and territorial as all hell. If there are three men in this town I wouldn't mind having in my corner, it's those three. But not a one of the three likes me much. Their wives are usually here...and I spend too much time here with them, scheduling more meetings than anyone rightly needs to have, just so I can catch a glimpse of Addison. They're suspicious.

I've been waiting for months for one of them to call me out on it and ask why I'm always here, but they haven't yet. Guess today is the day.

"Thanks," I mutter to Cami again and then tap on Riley's door.

"Come in!"

I push the door open.

Cash has a chair pulled up beside his pregnant wife, with her feet in his lap. Kasen's sprawled across the sofa across from Riley's desk, his long legs hanging off the end. Bentley's sitting in the floor near the window, toying with his guitar. They all look up at me, matching stoic expressions on their faces.

"Hey," Riley says, smiling at me. Her dark hair is thrown up in a scarf, her eyes dark beneath like she ain't been sleeping well. For a manager, Riley's young, still in her twenties. Doesn't stop her from being the best manager in the business. She's damn good at what she does, and everybody knows it. If she's terminating our contract today, I'll miss the hell out of her.

"Hey," I murmur, closing the door behind me. "Cash, Bentley, Kasen, good to see you again."

"You too," Cash says.

"Hey," Bentley mutters.

Kasen slowly sits up, making room for me to sit beside him. His dark eyes run over me, his lips pursed. Kasen is...Kasen. He's a wildcard. He's one of the few people who can get Addison to talk. Part of me appreciates him for it, the other part wants to shove his head up his own ass for it. If he didn't love his wife the way he does, that latter part would have won months ago. But he's obsessed with his wife, and he's one of the few people who can get Addison talking.

I eat up every word that spills from those sweet lips.

"We're here to guilt you into participatin' in Riley's new pet project," he announces, scrubbing a hand down his face. "But my baby is sick, my wife is pregnant, and I'm too fucking tired to play along, so surprise. You're doin' a charity benefit with me and Bentley on Wednesday. You aren't allowed to back out. It's been a done deal for like three months now. She just conveniently forgot to mention some pertinent fuckin' information."

"Kasen!" Riley growls, flinging a pen at his head.

I snatch it before it smacks me in the forehead.

"Sorry," she mutters, turning to grimace at me before she goes right back to scowling at him. Her gray eyes flash with annoyance. "I like you so much better when Olivia is here to make you behave."

"You're the one who made me come in for this shit," he retorts.

"Did not."

"Uh, yeah. Your exact words were 'Kasen, I need you to come help convince Clayton to do this charity benefit'," he says, pitching his voice high in an imitation of Riley. "I'm tired. You get what you get."

"Why do people even like you? You're so annoying," Riley complains.

"Because I'm hot, I play guitar, and I know how to change a diaper." Kasen smirks at her. "You love me too."

"She's going to murder you in your sleep one day," Bentley mutters, shaking his head.

"Nah," Kasen drawls. "She'd see me naked and die of shock."

"Or horror," Riley retorts, turning up her nose at him.

Cash scowls at the thought of his wife seeing Kasen naked.

"What charity benefit am I supposed to be working?" I ask, knowing they'll keep pecking at each other if I don't speak up. Riley and Kasen bicker like siblings. They love each other like siblings too. Once they get going, they keep going. Usually, I find it entertaining. Not today. Addison isn't here and I'm like a junkie in need of a fix.

"It's the American Cancer Society thing we discussed," Riley says. "The one in Chattanooga."

"Okay," I say, still not understanding why they're all here to guilt me into doing a show I already agreed to do. Riley knows her shit so I don't ask a whole lot of question when she books me for these things. If there's something she ain't telling me, maybe I should start asking more questions during all these meetings instead of zoning out to fantasize about Addison.

"Tell him the part you definitely didn't share," Bentley says.

Riley scowls at him like he's Kasen.

"It's a gala," Kasen says before she can. "Rich white men and their horny housewives."

"Suits and ties," Bentley grumbles, strumming a diminished seventh as if to punctuate his sentence with the dissonant chord.

"It won't be that bad," Riley says, rolling her eyes at them.

"You won't even be there," Kasen reminds her. "And it will be that bad. It'll be full of women trying to flirt with us and men tryin' to make deals with us. Which is why you waited until the eleventh hour to spring that detail on us."

"You don't need me there. Cami will be there."

"They better not be mean to my wife," Bentley growls, heat in his eyes. He's protective over his wife. Cami is beautiful, but people can be judgmental dicks. They talk about her size like it's their business. It's all jealousy and pettiness, coming from people who don't possess even a tenth of the grace and talent Cami has. Bentley can't stand it when anyone treats her badly. I don't blame him.

"I was thinking about sending Addison to help too," Riley says, her tone carefully casual.

I send a sharp look in her direction. She's watching me but trying not to let me know it. She's shit at subterfuge. I see right through her and that innocent expression. Does she know I have a thing for Addison or is she just guessing?

I can't tell.

"Addison don't like talking to people," I mutter, unable to stop myself. Not only do I want to fuck her until she's addicted to my cock, but I also want to protect her from any and everything that makes her anxious or frightens her. She isn't going anywhere if going will make her uncomfortable.

"She talks to me," Kasen says.

Possessive jealousy roils in my guts at the reminder.

"That's because you never shut up," Riley mutters to him before looking at me again. "It'll be good for her. She needs experience working events, plus we can use any photographs she takes for promotional purposes."

"Cami wouldn't mind having the company," Bentley says, still tinkering with his guitar. I'm not sure what he's doing with it. He's not tuning it and he's not really playing it. He just keeps running his hands over the strings. Maybe composing something new?

"Olivia will be there too."

"Addison can be your assistant, Clayton," Riley suggests.

I narrow my eyes, suspicious as hell. They didn't bring me here to guilt me into this event. They already knew I'd say yes even if it means dealing with the people who wouldn't have pissed on me if I was on fire three years ago. I've never refused to do an event for charity, no matter how highbrow. Which means I'm here because they know I have a thing for Addison. I'm just not sure if they're trying to help me out here or if they're trying to get me to fess up.

Don't they know they're tempting the devil here?

"Don't need an assistant," I growl, pissed that they're offering her up like a sacrifice, oblivious to how desperate I am. She's a little virginal lamb...and I'm the big, bad wolf, desperate to cull her from the herd so I can feast on her. I'll eat her alive, dirty her all up, and not regret a second of it. And they're making it so fucking easy for me.

"She'll do great," Riley says.

"She's a teenager."

Stop me, Riley. Goddammit.

"She's nineteen," Kasen points out, real fucking unhelpfully.

I know she's nineteen. She's been nineteen for three months, seventeen days. If I knew what time she was born, I'd know that math too. Every waking moment, I'm thinking about her. It's wrong and fucked up and I can't stop myself. And they're dangling her in front of me like a steak in front of a starving dog.

"I don't have time to babysit her," I growl, pissed beyond belief. Pissed because they're pushing. Pissed because they know my secret. Pissed because it doesn't change a damn thing. I still want her so badly I ache. Christ, I *ache.* "She'll just be in the way."

A soft gasp from the doorway stops my heart. Mid-beat, it just stops.

I jerk my head in that direction, already knowing she's there. And she is. Looking so tantalizingly sweet in her oversized sweater and leggings. The teal sweater hangs off one shoulder, revealing her smooth skin. The little dip in her collarbone has me ready to gnash my teeth in frustration that I don't know exactly what she tastes like right there. Her hair is down, her beautiful eyes bright. Those pouty lips are parted, shock and hurt stamped into every delicate line of her face.

Fuck. I hurt her.

No, little one. No.

My heart restarts, slamming against my ribcage in a powerful thud of protest before it snaps in half.

"Addison, I—"

"I may only be nineteen, but I am not a child and I do not need a babysitter," she growls at me, cutting Riley off. Her sweet voice shakes with emotion, with anger. She's speaking to me. First time in six long months. And my dick is hard, straining against my zipper, aching. She's pissed. Hurt. And I'm so hard it's torture.

She holds my gaze, her little chin jutting out, her shoulders square, her posture perfectly rigid. Pink creeps into her cheeks. Those eyes scorch me with hellfire. She's so damn beautiful in her fury, so damn vulnerable in her pain.

I'm sorry, little one.

"If Riley wants me to go to Chattanooga, I'm going," she says, those beautiful eyes daring me to gainsay her.

And I should. If I were stronger, I would. I'd tell her there's not a chance in hell that she's going anywhere with a man like me. But I'm weak. Christ, I'm so fucking *weak* when it comes to her. I'm going to consume her. Ruin her. When it's my time to stand in front of St. Peter and account for my sins...this will be the one that gets me cast into hell. And I won't even be sorry about it.

I dip my head in a nod, sealing her fate, and my own.

"Clayton."

I pause half-way to the elevator, waiting for Cash to catch up with me. He's got something to get off his chest. I owe him the opportunity to unload it. I saw him watching me after Addison stomped out. She wasn't at her desk when I left. It's killing me that I hurt her feelings.

Truth be told, I expected Kasen to be the one having this conversation. He was not happy that I hurt Addison's feelings. That makes two of us. My heart is trying to rip itself in two. I shouldn't be the one hurting her when all I want to do is love her.

I don't see her as a child. I *know* she doesn't need a babysitter. I was trying to save her. Looks like I might have accomplished it in a way I never intended, never wanted. She never should have had to hear those words from my lips. I never should have said them.

It's more proof that a girl like her deserves a hell of a lot better than a man like me.

"I'll walk with you," Cash mutters once he catches up to me.

I jerk my chin in a nod and head for the elevator.

We wait in silence.

Cash is cut from a different cloth. Most billionaires are exactly like Kasen and Bentley described. Old, white, thinking their shit don't stink while the fumes coming from it choke the world. Cash ain't like that. For one, he's young, early forties. For two, I don't think the man even owns a suit. For three, he spends as little time rubbing elbows with high society and counting his money like Scrooge McDuck as he possibly can.

He's a straight shooter, tells you like it is, and doesn't much care if you like him or not. He does what he thinks is right. And I'm guessing he's not too thrilled about sending Addison on the road with me, even with Kasen, Bentley, and their wives there. Can't say I blame him for that one, but he had time to speak his piece already. I'll let him say what he has to say out of respect for him and Riley. But there will be no warning me off Addison. Not now.

It's far, far too late for that.

"Addison means a lot to Riley," he finally says as the elevator shudders to life. He doesn't look at me, just stares straight ahead at the chrome doors.

I grunt, not sure what he expects me to say.

"She's family."

I shove my hands into the pockets of my black jeans.

"Anything happens to her, and we're going to have problems."

"You mean anything like me." It's not a question. We both know what he means. If I put my dirty hands on that pretty body, I'm going to answer to him. "You want to look out for her, be the good guy you are, that's cool," I mutter. "I respect that. Hell, I respect you. Takes a hell of a man to stand behind his woman the way you do with yours. But just so it's clear to you and anyone else who thinks about interfering, Addison is mine. She's been mine for the last seven and a half months. Try to come between us, and we're going to have problems."

He turns a calculating eye on me, his expression stoic. "So it's like that."

"It's been like that. You didn't know?"

After that meeting, I think it's pretty clear that everybody knows how I feel. That they've been aware for a while now that I come here for reasons that ain't necessarily right. I tried to save her from me. It just hurt her. I'm not doing that anymore.

The elevator slides to a stop, bouncing softly as the cables pull taut. The doors slide open.

I step forward to exit, and then pause, thrusting my boot between the doors to keep them from closing again. "Ain't nothing going to hurt that girl while I have breath in my body," I mutter, not sure why I say it. I don't owe him an explanation. But Addison Kissinger is mine. If she needs someone to protect her, it'll be me, not Cash Jamison. "I'll put down anything that tries."

"Fair enough," he mutters, still watching me. "Just know, if you fuck it up, you answer to me. I imagine you'll be answering to Kasen and Bentley too."

"Noted."

He eyes me for another minute, his expression inscrutable. He didn't make his money playing it safe or backing down. He's a hard-ass when he needs to be, ruthless. But I was cut from the same cloth. Nothing much intimidates me. After the shit I've seen and done in my life...well, we both know there's a reason we're having this conversation now and it ain't because I've been a choir boy.

I've sinned every which way but right. Drugs, guns, booze, I supplied them all...probably ran more drugs over the border than could fit in a ship. But I did my time, paid my penance, and moved on. My past is my past, lived a lifetime ago. Can't change it now or pretend it away, but I am who I am now. And it's not who I was then. But that cold, calculating motherfucker? The one capable of all manner of fucked up, back-alley bullshit?

He may be quiet, but he ain't dead.

Cash Jamison knows it. I'm guessing he knew it before the ink ever dried on my contract with his wife. Hell, he probably knew everything about my past the minute he and Riley stepped over the threshold into my bar three years ago.

He jerks his chin in a nod.

I step out of the elevator so we can both be going about our days.

"She's in love with you," he says before they slide closed. "That's why she doesn't talk to you."

I whip my head around to look at him, see the corner of his lip turned up in a grin, and then the doors close between us.

"Motherfucker," I curse, shocked. Addison has a thing for me?

Ah, little one. You shoulda run when you had the chance.

Chapter Three

Addison

"Hey. You okay?" Cami asks, placing her hand on my shoulder on her way across the office.

I pull my hands away from my face to look up at her. I can tell by the look on her face that she already knows what happened. Word travels fast around here. I didn't say anything when I left Riley's office. I just went to hide in the bathroom until I was sure Clayton was gone.

"Fine," I lie. The smile wobbles on my face and then collapses. I'm not fine.

Even though I've been telling myself for months that I don't stand a chance with him, hearing it from his lips still broke my heart into little pieces. I never imagined I would have to hear him say he thinks I'm just a kid in front of a room full of people I respect. When he let me down easy in my head, there wasn't an audience to my humiliation. It was private.

I'm sad and I'm angry and my heart is shattered into tiny pieces. He thinks I'm some little girl, that I'll get in his way. He's wrong. I may be small. I may be young. But I'm *not* a child in need of a babysitter. I don't get in the way. If he thinks I'm going to back out of going, he has another think coming. I'm going with him, just to prove to him that he's wrong about me.

I feel so stupid for hoping that maybe he saw me differently than most people do. That he was nice to me because he liked me. Finding out he's only nice to me out of pity stings.

Cami scrutinizes my expression, biting her bottom lip. "I don't know if I should say anything or not," she says after a moment, clearly worried about whatever it is.

"If you're going to tell me that I'm naïve for even entertaining the possibility that he could want me, you don't have to say it," I say with a sigh, staring at my hands. My nails gouged my palms, leaving crescent-shaped indentions. I'm not sure when it happened. I guess before I left from Riley's office like a coward. "I think he made it clear enough."

"That's not what I was going to say," she says, frowning at me. "You aren't naïve. Okay, that's not true. You are naïve, but that's not a bad thing, Addy. You see the good in people and in every situation. You see the world as it should be and live your life as if it is that way. That's not wrong and it doesn't make you somehow less than anyone else."

I know that, but I don't think the rest of the world agrees with me. I'm too young, too naïve, too quiet, too timid. I'm always *too much* of the wrong things. I've heard it my whole life. Until Laney, I didn't have many friends. I never dated or went out to parties. What I know about men, I learned from books and movies.

I'm a nineteen-year-old virgin who has never been kissed. Until I met Clayton, I never *wanted* to be kissed. All the girls in school talked incessantly about boys and sex. Even Laney had a crush on Weston and wondered what it would be like. No one ever interested me enough to wonder. Until Clayton. He's the only man I've ever wanted, the only one who has ever made my heart race or my entire body ache to be touched.

Now, I'm *too much* of something for him, too.

"What I was going to say is that I've been where you are," Cami says, her voice soft, "thinking Bentley was so far out of my league, it was laughable. If we were in the same room, I hid. I was so convinced that someone like him could never be with someone who looks like me. I wasted a lot of time that we could have spent together."

"That's different."

"How so?"

"Because Bentley is in love with you," I mumble, twisting my hands together. "Clayton pretty much confirmed that I'm just a little girl in his eyes. He thinks I need a babysitter." I scowl at the word. No one has had to babysit me since I was eleven.

"So, what are you going to do about it?" Riley asks, popping up out of nowhere. She waddles across the office toward me and Cami, loaded down with a stack of files. She drops them on the edge of my desk, placing her hands on her hips. It pulls her dress tight over her belly.

What *am* I going to do about it? Part of me wants to curl up and cry. The biggest part of me wants to do that. Because the biggest part of me is a coward. And that's the only side of me that Clayton has ever seen. The timid girl who can't even speak to him. But I'm more than that.

Maybe it's time to stand up for myself and show him that I may be timid, but I'm not a coward and I'm not a child. I may be young. I may be small. But I'm a woman. If he can't see that, I'm just going to have to show him.

"I'm going," I say, looking between Cami and Riley, reaffirming my declaration in the office.

"Duh," Riley says, smiling at me. "Of course you're going."

"I'm going to prove to him that I'm not a little kid."

Riley's smile widens.

"He likes you," Cami blurts.

I look at her.

"I'm serious, Addy," she says, no doubt reading my expression. "As soon as he walks in the door, he starts looking for you. If you aren't at your desk, he gets grumpy. Last time Kasen made you laugh, he actually growled."

"She's not lying," Riley says. "I never said anything because I wasn't positive until today...but he watches you almost as much as you watch him. Why do you think he wears the sunglasses?"

"I..." I stop and shrug. He's always worn them. I guess I just assumed he liked sunglasses.

Maybe I am a naïve little girl. People don't just wear sunglasses in the middle of a building for no reason.

"He thinks no one will notice him staring at you if he wears them," Riley says.

Little seeds of hope bloom in my chest, sprouting so quickly I struggle to stamp them out. I don't need to get my hopes up. He may like me as a person, but he made it pretty clear that he sees me as a kid.

"He thinks he's not good enough for you," Cami says, her voice soft.

"Right," I snort. "He's gorgeous, talented, every woman on the freaking planet wants him, and he makes millions. I'm a nineteen-year-old virgin who still sleeps with the light on and is too anxious to talk to 99.9 percent of the population."

"You sleep with a light on?"

"I ran away from a slumber party when I was eight and got lost in the woods," I mumble. "I was out there all night before someone found me. I don't like being in the dark."

"Addison," Cami whispers, her face falling.

Cami is the sweetest person I've ever met. She genuinely cares about everyone. It's one of the reasons it's so easy to talk to her. She never judges me no matter what I say.

"You better not cry!" Riley shouts at Cami, looking mildly horrified at the thought. "I'm pregnant. If you cry, I'm going to cry. And then Cash is going to have a meltdown."

"I'm not going to cry!" Cami huffs even though her eyes are bright with moisture.

"Neither of you are allowed to cry," I say to both of them. If they cry, I'll cry. And I already promised myself I wouldn't do that. "It was a long time ago. Besides, my point was that he could have anyone. Women literally throw him their panties when he's on stage. There's no way he thinks I'm too good for him."

"He was in prison." Riley gasps as soon as the words leave her lips and then slaps her hand over her mouth, her gray eyes wide.

Cami blinks, clearly shocked.

"I shouldn't have said that," Riley whispers, guilt stamped all over her face. "It's not my story to tell and it was a long time ago. Clayton is a *good* man who made mistakes and has worked hard to overcome them. Please don't judge him because of what he did a decade ago."

"I would never do that," I promise, reaching out to squeeze her hand. "Besides, I already knew."

"You did?" Riley gapes at me. "How did you know that? We worked our butts off to bury it."

"Um..." I blush, avoiding her gaze. "He has a tattoo on his arm, a clock face without hands. It's a common prison tattoo." I leave out the part about me Googling it to find out what it meant, hoping she won't ask. I don't really want to have to confess that I spend an unhealthy amount of time Googling him.

Cami joins Riley in gaping at me.

"The amount of random knowledge you possess is mildly terrifying," Riley mutters, shaking her head.

I breathe a little sigh of relief, glad I don't have to confess to researching his tattoos. Him saying I need a babysitter was humiliating enough, thanks. No way do I want to admit that I'm so in love with him I can catalogue every tattoo he's ever revealed. I can't help it though! I can't stop thinking about him. He's stuck in my head like a song.

"I don't even remember what we were talking about now," Riley says.

"Pregnancy brain," Cami teases her. "We were almost to the part where you tell Addison to make him see her as a woman instead of as a little girl so he gets over this whole thinking he's not good enough for her thing and they can get to the happily-ever-after part."

"Right," Riley says, pushing the sleeves of her dress up like she's getting ready to do manual labor or something when, let's be honest here, none of us have ever done manual labor in our lives and would probably die if we tried. "You're going to Chattanooga with him, and you're going to make him squirm."

"No," I say with a shake of my head. "I'm not going to make him squirm. I'm going to bring him to his knees."

"Hallelujah!" Riley shouts.

Cami collapses in a fit of giggles.

Even I laugh.

There's a reason I love working here.

"I just have one question."

"What?"

"Um, how exactly do I do that?" I ask, blushing. "I've never..."

"Tried to seduce a man?" Riley suggests.

"Yeah." I swallow hard. "I've never even been on a date."

Her eyebrows shoot skyward. "Not even one date?"

I shake my head.

"Not even a kiss under the bleachers?"

I shake my head again, hiding my eyes so I don't have to see the pity in theirs.

"I never dated before Bentley," Cami says. "He was my first everything."

"Cash was mine too."

"Really?" I peek up at them again.

They both nod, and I know they aren't just saying it to make me feel better. They mean it. Which makes me feel a little better. I was beginning to feel like the only person

I know not destined for love or marriage or babies...three things I've always wanted desperately.

While other little girls were dreaming about being the President of the United States or actresses or astronauts, I dreamed about being a mom. My little brother is seven years younger than I am. My parents worked a lot, so I watched him a lot growing up. Taking care of him always made me so happy. I love kids, especially babies. I want at least five of them.

"You seduce him by being you," Cami says.

"Just wear something sexy while you do it," Riley suggests. "I don't think it's going to take very much to break him. He's been ready to snap for weeks."

"Longer than that," Cami says, giggling.

"Maybe smile at a few strangers," Riley says, tapping her bottom lip like she's really considering my options. "If Clayton is the man I think he is, that'll really drive him crazy. You won't even have to talk to them or flirt with them. Just smile."

Smile. Wear something sexy. Be myself.

And if he still doesn't see me as a woman?

Well, then I'll just have to come up with a Plan C.

"Maybe I should come home," Laney suggests, sounding worried.

"You're not coming home early," I huff at her, throwing myself down on my bed to stare at the ceiling. My room looks like a tornado hit it. There are clothes on every surface. I don't think I have any left hanging in the closet, but I finally picked a few outfits to take with me, including a dress for the gala.

I'm not really sure what rich people wear to charity benefits, but my mom loves to shop, so I have several good options. The one I picked to take is daring for me. It's a sleeveless high low dress that ends well above midthigh in front but is floor length in the back. It's royal blue and black, very bold. I don't know where my mom expected me to wear it, but I'm glad I have it now.

"Are you sure–?"

"Positive." As much as I miss Laney, she doesn't need to come home early. I want to do this on my own. Actually, I think I have to do it on my own. It's the only way to prove to Clayton that I'm a grown woman. I feel oddly...excited at the prospect of making him squirm a little bit. Even if Cami and Riley are wrong about how he feels about me—and I'm pretty sure they are—I still want to prove that I can do this.

We're leaving Wednesday morning. The guys will rehearse when we get there and then perform that night.

We'll come home on Thursday. Which means I have twenty-four hours to change Clayton's mind about me.

It's strange. I've been so afraid to open my mouth and speak to him for so long. Yet when he called me a teenager in need of a babysitter, I didn't freeze. The words didn't stick in my throat, threatening to choke me. They just spilled right out. I didn't even have to think about it.

I think I'm still a little bit angry because the thought of talking to him doesn't scare me right now either. He already thinks the worst of me. It takes the pressure off. No matter what I may say or do, his opinion of me can't really get any worse than it already is. I have one chance to change his mind and make him see *me*.

I can't afford to waste it being anxious and timid and awkward and afraid.

"I kind of want to strangle him with his own guitar string," Laney mutters.

I smile. Not so long ago, I wanted to strangle Weston with his own skate strings for her.

My phone beeps with an incoming call.

"I have another call, hang on."

I pull the phone from my ear and then frown at the number. It's not familiar to me but it's too late for it to be a telemarketer. I swipe to answer.

"Hello?"

No one says anything.

"Hello?"

"Addison."

As soon as I hear his voice, I almost drop the phone. My heart thumps hard and then starts racing. Holy crap. It's Clayton. Clayton Devine is calling me.

"How did you get my number?" I blurt and then immediately cringe. The question is accusatory and a little hostile.

"Riley," he growls.

"Oh."

We sit in silence for a moment. It's so tense, it practically crackles down the line.

"Can-"

"We're leaving first thing in the morning," he says at the same time. "I'll be there to pick you up at ten."

"What?" I sit upright, shock rolling through me. "We're not leaving until Wednesday morning. Tomorrow is Tuesday."

"We're leaving tomorrow," he growls.

"I..."

"I'll be there at ten."

"Okay," I whisper.

He hesitates for a long moment.

I reach for something to say, but my mind is so busy panicking that I can't think.

"Sweet dreams, little one," he says before I can figure out how to form words and forge them into coherent speech, his voice somehow soft as velvet and gritty at the same time.

"Goodnight, Clayton."

He makes a noise, almost like a groan, and then disconnects.

"We're leaving tomorrow," I blurt as soon as I swap back over to Laney's call. "He just freaking called and said we're leaving in the morning. And I think I'm riding with him because he said he'll be here at ten to pick me up."

Oh, sure. *Now* I form sentences!

"Whoa," Laney says.

"I can't ride with him!"

"Why are you yelling?" she asks.

"I don't know!" I fling myself backward again, only to sit right back up. "What am I going to do in the car with him for two hours? Why are we leaving tomorrow?"

"Did you ask him that?"

"No. I forgot."

I can practically hear her head shake but she doesn't laugh at me.

"I'm going to text him and ask." I hesitate. "Should I text him?"

"Yes!" Laney laughs this time.

I take a deep breath, trying to get myself together. This is war. Okay, maybe not war. But this is serious business. I quickly type out a text asking why we're leaving tomorrow and then hit send before I can talk myself out of doing it.

"Sent. I guess I need to finish packing," I mutter. "I'll text you later."

"Tell him if he makes you cry, I'm making his life a living hell," Laney says.

I smile. Laney doesn't have a mean bone in her body, but I know she means it. She's fierce when she needs to be. She actually turned Weston down in front of an entire arena full of people three times in a row. She says I'm a bad ass, but really, she's the one with giant testicles. She always has been the brave one of the two of us.

"And Addy? Have fun," she says, her voice serious. "You deserve to be with someone who will make all of your dreams come true, someone who sees you for the powerful, beautiful woman you are. Don't forget that."

"I won't," I promise before we say goodbye and disconnect. I stare at my phone for a moment, waiting to see if Clayton is going to text me back. He read my message. I have the receipts. But he still hasn't responded.

I huff a breath and drop my phone before hopping up to finish packing. Even though I'm pretty sure I'm going to be the only one seeing my underwear, I take an inordinately long time picking out several pairs of panties and a couple bras. Most of what I own are feminine more than sexy, but Laney talked me into buying a few sets that are whatever comes after daring. I quickly shove all of them into my bag before I can talk myself out of it, and then zip it up, leaving all the cute panties where they're at.

By the time I finish packing and crawl into bed, it's almost midnight.

My heart stalls when I go to plug in my phone and see that Clayton texted me back. And then I read it and my eyes narrow on my phone.

Clayton: Why? Is it a problem?

"Jerk," I mutter.

This time, I leave him on read.

Chapter Four

"Jesus fucking Christ," I growl, staring at Addison when she flings open the door of her apartment at exactly 10 a.m., looking like my own personal idea of heaven. I'm not nearly awake enough to deal with her looking so edible. Nor am I awake enough to properly appreciate the way she scowls at me like I'm the devil, or how badly I want to spank her sexy little ass for it.

Her black hair is shiny and looks soft, making me want to feel it wrapped around my fist while my mouth is seamed to hers. Her pouty lips are stained red. I want to watch them form my name while I'm inside her, pumping so deep she'll feel me inside her every time she breathes.

Her thin white t-shirt hangs off one shoulder like her sweater did yesterday, exposing her shoulder and collarbone. She's wearing a bra because I can see the dark fabric through her shirt, but there is no strap. There are holes in her jeans, exposing tantalizing flashes of her thigh and knee. She has the cuffs rolled up with pretty black heels on her feet.

She's too beautiful, and I barely slept last night. I couldn't stop thinking about her long enough to settle. She's pissed at me, and I don't blame her for that. I was an asshole yesterday, but she doesn't understand why. She's pure and innocent, like sunshine and fresh air. I'm smoke, waiting for the opportunity to cover her in my filth.

She asked why we were leaving early. I wanted to tell her that I want her alone so I can find out for myself if she sounds as sweet begging my name as I imagine. She never answered my question last night. I must have checked my phone fifty times, worried leaving today would be a problem for her. I want to spank her for leaving me on read.

"I'm ready," she says in that soft voice that haunts every dream I have. There's a little pout to it that's all too appealing. She's cute the way baby tigers are cute. Cuddly, playful...deadly without even realizing it.

Her gaze drifts over me, noting my ensemble. All black, like usual. It's not a fashion statement. It's practical. Stylists piss me off. They always want to change me. My clothes, my hair, my beard. No need to hire one to catalogue all the ways I'm *not quite country enough* if everything I wear looks the same.

Addison's gaze lingers on my glasses for a long moment, staring as if she's trying to see through them to the blood-shot, bruised eyes beneath. A little hint of challenge lurks in her baby blues, screaming that she's in the mood to cause me all kinds of trouble today. The same warning whispers from the stubborn tilt to her chin and the way her little fists clench against her thighs. My sweet little angel has a touch of the devil in her today.

That realization sets my blood on fire in my veins.

"I'll take your bag," I mutter, spying it just inside the door behind her. The sight of it makes me smile. The bag is light pink and black with her name in a fancy script across the front. It's feminine and cute without being in your face about it, exactly like the woman who owns it.

She shifts out of the way, allowing me to grab it.

A black and white cat pokes its head up from the couch and hisses at me.

"Hat Trick, behave," she scolds the cat.

"Hat Trick?" I cock a brow at the name, sliding the strap of her bag over my shoulder. It's lighter than I expected. She didn't pack much. And then I see the dress bag hanging on a hook on the closet door to the right and swallow hard. The dress is...Jesus Christ. The top is shimmery black and sleeveless, with a big bow at the waist and layers of fluffy blue fabric. She's maybe five foot four, but there isn't nearly enough fabric for it to cover all of her.

"It's a hockey thing. He's Laney's cat," she mumbles, grabbing the dress bag before I can tell her there isn't a chance in hell I'm letting her wear it.

The thought of anyone seeing her in it has possessive fury churning through me. I was in a motorcycle club for years, got into my fair share of fights. I never lost one, and I have no problem turning this gala into a ballroom brawl. No one looks at Addison except me, and they damn sure don't touch her. She's mine.

I grunt as she slips past me out the door, so close I can smell her cotton candy scent. She's sweet from head to toe. A coil of anticipation winds in my stomach, cinching my balls up tight. As soon as she lets me, I'm going to drown myself in her smell. I'll wear it every day until she orders me away from her. Everyone will know who she belongs to then.

I pull the door closed, turning to face her. She waits until I move out of the way to lock the door. I think she's trying to avoid getting too close to me, but I see her peeking at me out of the corner of her eye. When she notices me noticing, she scowls and stomps toward the parking lot.

I follow behind, grinding my back teeth at the sight of her ass in those jeans.

She comes to a dead stop when she sees my car. It's small, sleek, and fast as hell.

"It's an Aston Martin DBR1." I step up behind her, so close I know she feels me there.

She shivers, goosebumps rising on her neck where my breath touches it.

"It's one of five in existence."

"Is that supposed to impress me?" she asks, her back ramrod straight.

"Just wanted you to know that it still pales in comparison to you, little one." I step around her to put her bag in the trunk. Between my guitar equipment, our bags, and her dress, the trunk is full. If we weren't going out of town, I would have brought my bike. But I don't want her getting cold in the mountains, and she deserves to ride in style.

I don't need much in this life. My bike, my guitar, a good beer, and I'm satisfied. The car is the only luxury I've given myself since climbing the charts. I've given away millions. Everything else is just sitting there, collecting interest. When she's mine, I'm going to spoil her like the queen she is. She can have whatever she wants, do whatever she wants. That ripe little body will be draped in diamonds, wrapped in silk, and drowned in pleasure.

By the time I get her shit in the trunk, she's already in the car. I adjust my dick, already knowing it's futile. The car is small. I'm going to be breathing her in for the next two hours. I jacked the bastard raw last night, but he ain't going down anytime soon.

I smell her as soon as I open the door. I've never much cared for sweets. But you better believe, I'm going to feast on her like a dog.

She startles, dropping her phone when I slide in beside her.

Fitting in this car ain't easy for a guy my size. My old man used to want one, said if he ever won the lottery, this car is the first thing he'd buy. He had a thing for expensive cars and fast women. Despite his flaws, he was a good father. I bought this car for him.

He died while I was doing time. Never came to see me. He always warned me that he wouldn't, said if I didn't get my head out of my ass and got what was coming to me, I was on my own. I'm not mad at him for it. Hell, I don't blame him for washing his hands of me.

There aren't many laws I didn't break back then. Thought I was smarter than the law, that my so-called brothers would keep their word and have my back. The thing about criminals though...when they don't need you anymore, they find a way to deal with you. My number came up the day I helped the old lady of the Pres. escape. He beat the hell out of her. I gave her the money she needed to get their kid and go.

My next job was a setup.

I spent the first year of my sentence planning my revenge. Never did get it. By the time I got out, he was dead, and the rest of the club was scattered, most of them doing their own sentences. Karma works in funny ways.

It feels like a lifetime ago now. But I know I ain't done atoning for what I did back then.

Addison's lips twitch as I get comfortable.

"I see you laughing," I mutter, shaking my head at her.

She stops fighting it and giggles.

That sound. Christ, I want to hear that sound every day for the rest of my life. I want to be the reason she makes that sound. I thought hearing her say my name last night was heaven. I was wrong. Being the reason she's laughing tops it by miles.

"We can take my car," she says through her giggles.

"It's all good, little one."

Her giggles fade, her expression turning serious. Something like pain flashes in her eyes before she blinks it away, squaring her shoulders. "I'm not a little kid."

I grunt and start the engine. The car purrs to life, filling the strained silence between us. Addison is tense, clearly still pissed. And I shouldn't find it cute that she's mad. She'd probably kick my ass if she knew how beautiful I find her right now, with her eyes narrowed and her jaw set. But there isn't a time when part of me isn't in awe of how perfect she is from the top of her head to the tips of her toes.

"Never saw you as a kid," I mutter as I pull away from the curb. The problem isn't that I think she's a kid. That's never been the case. The problem is that I've always seen her as a woman, one far too good for the likes of me. She's got her whole life ahead of her. Don't think she'd feel the same about me if she knew how badly I fucked mine up long ago.

"You called me a teenager yesterday."

"You weren't supposed to hear that."

She huffs.

"I shouldn't have said it," I say when she doesn't speak.

"You said I need a babysitter."

Why is my dick hard because she's pouting? Jesus.

"You looked in the mirror lately, baby?" I ask, taking a left out of the parking lot. "You're too goddamn beautiful to be out in the world on your own. Men think all kinds of nasty shit when they see a sweet little thing like you."

"I..." Her pouty lips part and her voice fails her.

We ride in silence until we're well outside the Nashville city limits. I can practically see the wheels spinning in her mind, see her struggling to fit this new information into place with the little pieces she already has. I also see the instant she convinces herself I didn't mean what I said...and the instant she finally works up the courage to ask me.

"D-d-d..." She clenches her fists and takes a deep breath, lets it out on a slow exhale. "Do you think nasty...things?"

I take a second to appreciate how much it cost her to ask me that question. She's so shy, oblivious to the power she holds. One word from those lips, one tear from those pretty eyes...I'd be on my knees, pleading for mercy. She'll learn though. One day soon, she'll realize she holds every card in the deck. I can't wait for her to completely annihilate me with them.

"Do I think about nasty things when I look at you?" I ask, not sure she's ready to hear the truth. She's getting it anyway. "If you knew the things I've thought about doing to you, you wouldn't be sitting in that seat right now, little one. You'd have run in the other direction a long time ago."

Her thighs cinch together on the seat. Her breath expels in a trembling rush. The force of it jiggles her tits. Her pupils dilate, her expression dazed.

Jesus Christ. Looks like Cash might have been right. My little angel's been having bad, bad thoughts about me. The evidence of her arousal has cum dripping into my boxers. I shift on the seat, trying to make more room for my dick.

"And just in case it ain't clear enough," I mutter, unable to stop myself, "I haven't stopped looking at you once in the last seven months, Addison."

Her sweet little whimper is so soft anyone else probably would have missed it. Not me. I've been hyper-focused on her so long, I don't miss a sound she makes. And I already know, when she makes that sound while I'm inside her, I'll be giving her those babies she wants so badly.

"I-I'm not...I'm not running."

Despite me having glasses on, she seems to know exactly where my eyes are focused. Her gaze tangles with mine, determination lighting the blue depths with more hellfire. A whole inferno rages between us, roaring like a demon.

I jerk my chin in a nod and then glance away.

She settles back in her seat, shivering like she's cold. Her nipples aren't hard because of the bite in the air though.

I turn the heater up anyway, turn the radio on, and drive.

"Could you move a little faster?" I growl, glaring at the desk attendant at the hotel. He's maybe twenty-five, with slicked back hair and a cocky grin. He keeps looking at Addison. Every time she notices, she gives him a shy smile.

I'm man enough to admit that jealousy is eating me alive.

I want her smiling at me, not at Chad.

She fell asleep on the drive, looking all sweet and cuddly with her lips parted and her hands under the side of her face like a pillow. I wanted to snap a picture of her. Knowing she felt safe enough with me behind the wheel to sleep made me feel like a God.

It's funny, people have been screaming my name for three years and it never made me feel a tenth of the pride I feel knowing Addison was comfortable enough with me to fall sleep, trusting that she'd be safe. All those screams don't come close to matching the way it feels now that she's speaking to me. She mumbled my name in her sleep once. I'm not sure it was a good dream though because her little face scrunched up and she whimpered. My whole system lit up anyway.

My hand still tingles where I touched her face, trying to soothe her. It's like she really is made of magic. It dances in her aura and hums in her skin, infecting the air around her with that sweetness. As soon as I touched her, I felt it and never wanted to stop.

"Almost finished," Chad says, looking up to give Addison another grin.

She smiles back.

I knew when I picked her up that she was in the mood to give me trouble today. And I don't blame her for it. I hurt her feelings yesterday, made her feel like she's less than perfect. She can give me all the trouble she wants, but this smiling at Chad shit? Hell no.

I shift closer to her and tip my head down, so close I feel her hair tickling the side of my cheek. "You keep looking at him like that, I'm going to do something you'll regret."

"W-what?" she whispers, turning wide eyes in my direction.

"Stop fucking smiling at him," I growl.

There's definitely a little bit of the devil in my angel today. Her brows furrow, her baby blues flashing with irritation. It's the only warning I have before the pointy heel of her shoe digs into the top of my foot. Even through my boot, it hurts like hell. Which, I suspect, is exactly what she intended.

"Don't curse at me," she huffs and then removes her foot and takes a step away from me.

Chad hears her and looks up, glancing between us. His expression sours. "You're on the top floor," he says, sliding over the keycard to the suite. "The private elevator is on the left."

When I told Riley we were leaving today instead of tomorrow, she didn't seem surprised. She told me she'd have everything taken care of and for me to take care of Addison. I think she wanted to say something, but she didn't. I'm glad she booked us in the presidential suite though. It's more space than we need but I want to spoil Addison a little.

Between work and school, she's got so much on her plate. She deserves to be spoiled.

"Someone will bring your bags up," Chad says. "Enjoy your stay."

"Plan on it," I mutter, taking the keycard from him and then placing my hand on the small of Addison's back to lead her toward the elevator. She's bristling like an angry kitten, but she lets me lead her toward the private elevator.

As soon as we're on the elevator and the doors close behind us, she pulls away. I should let her go, but I don't. She's got my blood heated and my cock hard. Possessive jealous roils like storm clouds in my guts, screaming at me to claim her, make her submit.

I stalk her across the small space, not stopping until she's flat against the wall, her fists clenched, and her head tilted back with her eyes locked on my face. Her cheeks are flushed, her pupils dilated. She's turned on, practically squirming with the ache kicking up a fuss in her belly.

"Don't curse at me. It's rude," she growls, her sweet voice trembling.

"Stop flirting with Chad."

"I smiled at him, Clayton." She rolls her eyes, but I see the little flicker of guilt. She quickly stamps it out, giving me that look I'm coming to know so well. The one that spells trouble about eight different ways.

When she's working and things aren't going the way she expects, she gets this stubborn gleam in her eyes and refuses to give up no matter how many times she has to change things to make her plan work. The fact that she's wearing it now shouldn't have my dick hard enough to pound steel, but it does.

My shy little angel is gone.

In her place is a warrior, determined to make me see the error of my ways. She's going to make me fight for every inch, see her for the woman she is. Just thinking about all the ways she's going to give me trouble has me ready to tumble her to the floor and fuck the fight right out of her.

I shove my hands into my pockets to keep them away from temptation and then press close. As soon as I feel that sweet body against mine, my whole system lights up again.

She's so soft, so sweet. I can't wait to dirty her up, teach her why her nipples are so hard and she's trembling and squeezing those thighs together right now.

"You want to make me suffer for being an ass yesterday, baby?" I ask, skimming my nose down the side of her cheek. I inhale her like I'm starving for oxygen, greedy for her scent. Her body trembles, pressing those tits even harder up against me. My cock nestles against her belly, hard and unyielding, desperate for her to acknowledge him.

"N-n-no," she whispers. She makes that sound again, that fucking whimper. Jesus God. Ain't a man alive who wouldn't want to be where I am right now, ain't one who wouldn't want to be responsible for that sound coming from her lips.

"You do, and that's all right, baby. I'll play along. I'll let you make me as miserable as you need to make me until you're ready to forgive me for hurting you yesterday," I say, placing my lips next to her ear. She smells so good. I just want to drown in her. "Torture me. Break me. But don't flirt with another man or flaunt what belongs to me, little one. Because I got the devil in me too. And I ain't got no problems putting down anyone who tries to touch you."

"Clayton," she whispers.

"You hurting, baby?"

She bobs her head.

"Here?" I pull my hand out of my pocket, wedging it between her thighs. Her little cunt ain't even big enough to fill my hand, but the heat coming off it burns me alive. I'm going to imprint my dick in that little thing when I get inside it.

"Yes!" she sobs.

"Soon as you're done being mad, I'll teach you why," I murmur, planting my lips against the pulse beating like a drum in her throat. I touch my tongue to it, and then lick a line up to her ear, unable to stop myself. "Hope your daddy's ready to be a grandpa, little one, because I'll be making you a mommy just as soon as you let me in this sweet little thing."

She sobs my name this time. And it hurts. Christ, it *hurts* knowing she's hurting for me and I can't do a damn thing to make it better for her right now. But I can't. When I'm inside her for the first time, she'll know this thing between us is permanent, unalterable. She won't be mad, and she won't regret a single second of it. Until she knows beyond a shadow of a doubt that my heart beats for her and her alone, I'll endure the pain.

I grind the heel of my hand against her pussy, just to hear her sob my name again.

"You say my name so sweet. You gonna scream it just as sweet too?"

She whimpers again, stretching the bonds of my rapidly fraying self-control.

"Jesus ain't made a sweeter angel than you." I press my lips to the corner of her mouth, just enough to taste that pouty bottom lip of hers. "He should have taken better care with you, kept you out of my path. I'm going to eat you alive, Addison."

I flick my tongue out to touch her lips and then reluctantly tear myself away from her before I lose the ability to do it at all. One final look at her splayed up against the wall, all flushed and turned on and I'm running for the bathroom, already working at the fly of my jeans, desperate for relief.

I shout her name when I come all over my hand, hoping like hell she hears it.

Chapter Five

"How is it going with Clayton?" Riley asks, rabid curiosity in her voice.

"Um, it's going," I murmur, my cheeks heating even though she can't see me. I'm curled up on the bed in the room I picked out, avoiding Clayton. I love Riley, but I'm still trying to process what happened in the elevator. I'm not ready to share it yet.

I'm in serious trouble with him. The heart racing, palms sweating kind of trouble. He worked sexual voodoo on me and I still haven't recovered. Feeling his lips against my skin while his beard and mustache tickled me was heaven. My legs feel like rubber and I'm burning up. The ache in my center hasn't abated at all. I'm still reeling. It has me feeling...I don't honestly know.

Part of me knows he means what he said. The other part is still too afraid to hope.

I've been in love with him for so long, I think I'm afraid to let him in now. Especially after yesterday. What if he changes his mind? Decides I am too young for him? Too naïve?

He's a freaking superstar. It's hard to wrap my mind around the possibility that he wants me as badly as I do him. But I heard him in the elevator. I felt how his body responded to me. None of that was a joke or pretend.

I think he masturbated when he left the elevator. He cried out my name.

It made my entire body hurt for him even more.

"We made it to the hotel about an hour ago," I say, changing the subject.

"Good. There's not much for you to do today," Riley says, not prying. "The stage in the ballroom should be set up this evening. If you could run down and check on it tonight, that's all I really have for you today. Clayton was just antsy to get there."

"He likes to be prepared."

"Mmhmm," she says, a teasing note in her voice. "I'll let you go with that, but don't think you aren't spilling the beans when you get back."

"We'll talk then," I promise.

"Is he being good to you?"

"Yes," I whisper.

"Good. He better be," she growls, making me smile. Riley loves Clayton, but I think she would kick his butt for me if he weren't being nice to me. She's protective. It's one of the reasons her artists love her so much. She truly cares about them and their careers. She does what is genuinely best for them, even if it means saying no to lucrative deals.

"Kasen's band will be there in the morning to set up," she says, switching back to business mode. "We've already arranged for them to back Clayton. They've played with him before, so they already know most of his stuff. Once they run through it tomorrow, they should be good to go."

"Okay. What time is rehearsal tomorrow?"

"One," she says. "Cami and Bentley will be there in an hour or two. Cami will run the show, you're just there to help keep Clayton in line. He doesn't handle fancy pants rich people any better than Kasen or Bentley." I can practically hear her eyes roll. "I swear, I don't know why I put up with the three of them."

"You love them."

"Don't tell them that."

"Promise," I say, smiling. They already know. She thought about quitting when she first found out she was pregnant, but Cash talked her into staying. I've never seen Clayton as relieved as he was when she broke the news to him.

"For today, just have fun and relax!" she orders me. "Seduce that man of yours."

"Working on it," I mutter, which makes her giggle. My seduction plan is not going so well. Actually, it's not going at all. He's been doing most of the seducing. And smiling at Chad pissed him off and made me feel horribly guilty. I think Riley and Cami gave me bad advice, so I'm just going to do things my way. I'm not ready to wave the white flag just yet. The thought of making him crazy is...honestly kind of thrilling. He told me to torture him, to break him.

What does it mean that I want to do that? That I want to make him as crazy as possible? No one has ever touched me like he did in the elevator or made me feel like he did. I want to do the same thing to him, see him crumble for me. Not because I'm angry at him or hurt. I think I'm mostly over what happened yesterday. But because, for the first time in my life, I feel sexy, desired...powerful.

I want to use that newfound power, see how wild I can make him.

I feel him standing in the doorway before I see him. His presence is so...absolute. People notice him, not because he's a superstar, but because it's so impossible to miss him. He's larger than life, dangerously hot and fiercely masculine. Even before he opens his mouth, people notice him.

There aren't many men like him in the world. At least none that I've ever seen before. It's easy to see why women go crazy over him. He's raw sexuality, capable of working a sort of magic that's irresistible.

"Lunch is here," he says in that same rough growl that heats my blood. He leans up against the doorjamb, his arms crossed over his chest so the rose tattoo on his forearm is visible. He's not wearing his sunglasses anymore. His forest green eyes lock on me, searing in their intensity.

"I'll let you go," Riley says. "Have fun. Bye!"

She hangs up before I can say anything back. I set the phone on the bed beside me, sitting up to face Clayton. "You ordered lunch?"

"Thought you might be hungry," he says, holding out a hand to me.

"Oh."

"Come here, little one."

I crawl from the bed and cross the room to him, letting him take my hand. As soon as he touches me, my heart speeds up. Energy or desire or *something* sizzles against my skin, humming like charged high voltage lines. It feels incredible, peaceful and exciting at the same time. My body seems to know him, crave him. As soon as he touches me, my mind settles.

His hand is so much bigger than mine and rough, but he laces our fingers together gently, as if he's afraid to hold me too tightly. He doesn't say anything else as he leads me through the suite. I've never seen luxury like this before. Between the two bedrooms, the living room, full kitchen, and the giant bathroom, the suite probably takes up half the top floor of the hotel. It's beautiful.

My steps falter when we reach the living room. A small table is set up in front of the balcony doors. The mountains in the distance are capped with snow. The city sprawls around the hotel, with roads twisting and coiling like a snake. A single candle burns in a silver candlestick on top of the table, with covered dishes on each side. There's a vase of vivid orange flowers next to the candle.

"You did all this for me?" I ask, staring up at him in shock.

"When are you going to learn?" he asks, shaking his head at me. His expression is so somber and serious, so patient. "There ain't a whole lot in this world I wouldn't do for you."

My knees get weak as he burrows a little deeper into my heart, claims another piece of it. For someone who doesn't usually say very much, he's awful good at saying just the right things. It's not an act either. With some men, it's cheesy lines, said because they're after something.

Not Clayton. There's no deception in him, no suave player or carefully planned endgame. With him, what you see is what you get. He's a simple conundrum, so easy to figure out and yet steeped in mystery at the same time.

"Come on," he murmurs again, tugging me across the room. He pulls my chair out for me like a gentleman, standing so close I feel the heat coming off his body. I just want to melt into him.

I reach deep for all the courage I can muster and press back against him. His body is hard against mine, and so much wider. He's so dang *big*. And hard. God, his body is incredible. He never reveals much of it, but it's impossible to miss all those muscles.

A lot of stars get ahead by stripping down. Not him. He's probably been asked a thousand times to pose shirtless, but he's refused every one of them. His music speaks for him, not his body. There are no gimmicks or tricks, no autotune or backup dancers or fancy sets. He's the epitome of that old country soul, unflinchingly real, humble, and modest.

He slides an arm around my waist, splaying his hand across my abdomen. I feel his lips at the side of my throat, feel the way his breath dances against my skin. His beard tickles me, making me yearn for things I barely understand. My belly flutters beneath his palm, aching to feel his bare hand there.

He's erect, painfully so. I can feel it nestled against my butt. I press back further, shifting against him. He's so hard. I've never seen a penis outside of the few times I tried to watch porn. They didn't seem quite this big. I can't help but wonder what it would be like with him.

He's so sweet to me sometimes and so gentle, but I think he's telling me the truth when he says he's got a little of the devil in him. I can't imagine him being sweet and flowery in bed. He's dominant, possessive, wicked. I think he will be in bed too.

His breath rasps in his throat, shaking slightly. A growl rumbles there too. His hand tightens on me as he grinds his hips into my bottom, letting me feel him. The heat he sent racing through me in the elevator comes roaring back to life.

"You're playing with fire," he warns me.

"Maybe I want to burn." Maybe I want him to burn too.

"You are going to torture me, aren't you?" He buries his face in my throat and groans. He doesn't sound mad about it though. He sounds...turned on. "Go ahead then. Ruin me, baby girl."

"I want something."

"You can have anything."

"A date."

He freezes before untangling himself from me.

A fissure opens in my heart, threatening to split it wide open, right down the middle. He's going to tell me no. Whatever this is...whatever he wants from me...I don't think he wants anyone to know about us. He wants it to be a secret.

He turns me to face him, unrelenting. I resist but it's futile.

"Look at me, Addison."

I fix my eyes on his chin.

He sighs and puts his hand under my jaw, tilting my head back until I'm forced to meet his gaze. I can't read his expression. There's heat there, a little amusement too. And something soft.

"You want me to take you out? Want people to see us together?"

"It was a stupid idea," I mumble even though I do want that. Not because he's Clayton Devine, country music superstar. But because he's Clayton Devine, the man who crams himself into a tiny sports car for two hours just so I can ride in luxury. Because he's the man who rents a ridiculously expensive suite for me and buys me flowers for lunch, just because he thinks I deserve them. Because he's the man who gets jealous when I smile at anyone who isn't him, yet thinks I should run in the other direction from him.

I would be so dang proud to be on the arm of that man.

"You think I don't want to be seen with you?" he asks, his voice soft.

I shrug.

"I'll take you anywhere you want to go, anytime you want to go," he murmurs. "Ain't a man alive who wouldn't want to take you out and show you off. But you sure you want to be seen with me?"

I freeze, shocked by the thread of uncertainty in his voice. It would have probably gone unnoticed by anyone who wasn't completely obsessed with every word he speaks and every sound he makes. It's almost imperceptible. But it's there, just like it is in his music. He's ashamed of himself. I don't understand why.

"I wasn't a good man before I met you," he says, swallowing hard. "Done a lot of things I'm not proud of doing, hurt people sometimes."

"You were in prison."

It's his turn to be shocked. He blinks.

"No one told me," I hurry to say, not wanting him to think Riley divulged his secret. I mean, she kind of did, but I already knew and she felt awful about it, so it doesn't count. "I...um, your tattoo. On your arm. The clock face without the hands? I got curious and looked it up one day. I know it means you were in prison."

He stares at me, not saying anything for so long I think he's mad. And then he expels a heavy breath. "Drug trafficking," he says, dipping his head to hide his eyes. "I did five years in federal for running drugs across the border."

"Oh. Did you...do them?"

"Hell no," he growls. "I never put that shit in my body." He meets my gaze again. "And before you go justifying that, thinking it somehow makes what I did less fucked up than it was, it don't. I may not have taken them, but I brought plenty of them into this country."

"Why?"

"It's a long story that don't end happy," he says, his expression making it clear he isn't going to answer that question, at least not right now. "You want me to take you out, I'll take you wherever you want to go. But you ought to know you deserve a helluva lot better than a man like me."

"You're wrong," I whisper.

"I'm not."

"Yeah, you are." I narrow my eyes, mad that he's talking badly about himself, that he thinks he's not good enough for me. "Everyone deserves forgiveness, Clayton. Even you. *Especially* you. You aren't the same person you were then."

"You're wrong," he says, pulling me into his arms. He plunges his hand into my hair, gripping it tight and pulling my head back. It doesn't hurt. It feels...good. Really good. "I may not do the shit I used to do, may even do a few good deeds now and again, but the man I was back then? He's still standing in front of you, baby girl. And he's dying to get his hand around your pretty throat while he's filling that little cunt full of his seed."

My lips part on a moan.

"Jesus." His gaze skirts over my face. "You like knowing that, don't you?"

"Y-yes."

"You shouldn't," he growls. "He don't deserve to kiss the pretty heels on your feet."

"Yes, he does. *You* do."

He growls a warning and then his mouth is on mine. His kiss is hot, possessive, full of lethal intent. He doesn't ease me into it. He kisses me like he wants me to know just how desperate he is for me, just how bad he wants to be for me. His beard abrades my skin, but it feels so dang good. I moan into his mouth, turn pliant in his arms.

His tongue touches mine, and I see heaven, taste it. He's cinnamon heat and steam, breathing fire into my lungs, into my soul. And I want to burn. Want it so bad I practically crawl up his body, plunging my hands into his hair. It's as soft as I always thought it would be.

His hands journey all over my bottom, boosting me up until my legs are around his waist and he's grinding against me, growling like a wild animal. Our mouths meet again and again, parting only long enough to take shallow breaths before we lock on one another again, both starving. Both desperate.

"Clayton," I moan, writhing in his arms in a pleasure so intense it borders on pain.

"Fuck," he growls. His mouth touches mine again, his tongue stroking deep. He backs off and bites my bottom lip, jostling me against his erection. "Knew you'd be hot for me when I got my mouth on you, but Jesus Christ, Addison, didn't know you'd feel this good in my arms."

"Me...me either," I gasp.

"How the hell am I supposed to stay out of this little thing when I can already smell how sweet it is?" He sounds mad, but the way he rocks me against him again is evidence to the contrary. "I can practically feel how wet you are for me."

"Clayton," I whimper, raking my nails down his back and then plunging my hands right back into his hair. I tug, trying to get him to put his mouth on me again.

"We gotta stop."

"No."

"Addison, baby..." He kisses me again, hard and deep. "Shit, we gotta stop. My phone."

I only hear it blaring through the room after he says it. It's loud, one of those annoying ringtones that come with the phone. I cry out in frustration.

"Shh, little one. Shh," he croons, planting kisses all over my exposed shoulder. "Promise I'll take care of you real soon, give you what you're hurting for."

"Promise?"

"Not even the devil himself could stop me," he growls. He means it.

It's enough...for now.

I reluctantly release my grip on his hair, stop grinding against the bulge in his pants. He keeps ahold of me for a minute, panting and staring at me like he's ready to say to hell with food and have me for lunch. But then his phone starts ringing again. He grits out a curse and slowly slides me down his body.

My feet land on the floor, but I feel like I'm floating five miles above it.

Lord, I think he's going to ruin me.

He waits until I'm steady on my feet and then yanks his cellphone from his pocket to answer it. "What?" he growls, not even checking to see who it is.

I giggle, unable to help it. He's like a grumpy little boy whose favorite toy was taken away. Except there's nothing little about him. He's all man, pissed off, turned on, ready to snap.

Maybe I'm not so bad at this seduction thing after all.

"Yeah, fine," he says to whoever is on the phone. "We'll be there." He listens for another minute and then disconnects before tossing the phone toward the sofa. It bounces on the cushions, landing face down.

He stands there for a long moment, eyes closed, taking deep breaths.

I start to ask if he's okay, but his eyes flash open, landing on me like I'm the prey he's been hunting through the jungle. His nostrils flare, so much heat banked in those green eyes they look like storm clouds, those ominous green ones that spell danger of the tornado variety. And then his expression softens, his lips crooking into that little boy grin that I love so much.

"Let me feed you," he murmurs, slipping his hand into mine. This time, I let him help me sit. He scoots my chair in and then brushes his fingertips across my shoulder.

I shiver.

"We're going out with Cami and Bentley and Kasen and Olivia tonight," he says.

"Oh. Um..."

"It's a triple date," he says, reading my mind. His eyes meet mine again. "You can change your mind."

I think he's speaking about more than me being seen in public with him. I think he's speaking about him, about us. He's giving me another out. Except I don't want it. Even if this ends with my heart broken into little pieces...I don't want out.

"What time should I be ready to go?"

He stares at me for a moment and then dips his head in a nod, silently admitting his defeat.

Chapter Six

I strum the final chords of the song I'm working on and then set my guitar aside to cross out a line in my notebook. The song is coming together, but that line doesn't fit. It's too...safe. Ain't nothing safe about the woman who inspired it. She's an angel, true enough, but she shines bright and hot enough to burn. That brightness has been searing me all day.

Taking my mouth off her was the hardest thing I've ever done. I want her naked beneath me, moaning for me more than I want my next breath. I also want to turn her little ass red for knowing about my past and still wanting me. It's blowing my mind that she knows and still isn't running in the other direction. That she thinks I'm worthy of her.

I'm not, of course. Never have been, never will be. But I'm not arguing. I may not be a smart man, but I ain't a dumb one either. If she's willing to accept me, I'm not sending myself away from her. Probably couldn't even if I wanted to do it. I'll take her on any date she wants to go on and spend every second of it proud as hell to be the man on her arm.

If heaven is real, I just visited it for lunch. She let me sit her on my lap and feed her. Never knew feeding someone from my own hand could be so damn satisfying but feeding her made me feel like a king. So did the way she kept smiling at me. Not those shy smiles she was giving Chad earlier, but big, bright ones that made those pretty eyes shine.

After lunch, she curled up on the couch with a book.

I sat beside her with the television on. Didn't watch it though. I couldn't take my eyes off her long enough to watch it. She kept giggling at whatever she was reading. Other parts made her blush and squirm and peek over at me. I have a feeling it was one of those dirty books she and Cami talk about sometimes.

She headed to her room two hours ago to get ready. I've been waiting for her for the last hour, but I'm not going to hurry her. She can take as long as she wants. I love that she's feminine and girly and loves pink and animals and dirty books and taking hour long showers. There's something so beautiful in how much joy she gets from the little things. I love how happy they make her.

I pick up my guitar and run through the song again, swapping out lyrics that don't feel right. It's closer but still not finished. It's missing something. I just can't figure out what.

"Wow," Addison whispers from the doorway when I set my guitar aside this time. "Did you just write that?"

"Been working on it a while," I mutter, flipping my notebook closed and then glancing up at her. "It's finally...Jesus Christ." My dick gets hard so fast my head spins. "What the fuck are you wearing, little one?"

"A dress."

If that's a dress, I'm a unicorn. The thing ties around her neck, with thin silver chains that hang between her breasts. The black fabric hugs every curve of her body, with a split up her right thigh, showing off one ridiculously long leg. She's changed into even taller heels than the ones she had on earlier. Her hair is all ruffled and her lips are bright red. She looks like pure sex.

She gives a little spin and I damn near whimper. The dress is backless. I can see the dimples above her luscious ass. I want to press my lips to them before I sink my teeth into those supple cheeks.

"You trying to get spanked?" I ask, rising to my feet. I prowl toward her across the room, helpless to do anything but move toward her. She's gravity, pulling me into her field of orbit.

She stands up straight, her top teeth sinking into her bottom lip as her gaze roves all over me. Her eyes darken like I'm the one dressed indecently even though I'm in the same thing I always wear, black on black. I like her looking at me like that though.

"I like my dress," she says when I slide an arm around her waist, pulling her up against my body.

"I'll be raw dogging you in the back of the bar for your first time if I gotta look at you in that all night, little one."

Her face scrunches up. "Raw...what?"

"Fucking you without a condom," I explain, fighting a smile. She's so damn innocent.

"Oh." Her wide eyes meet mine. "We can't do...that in a bar, can we?"

She looks excited by the suggestion, and I can't fight my smile this time. She's as curious as she is innocent, eager to explore. I don't know what I did to deserve a gift like her, but I'm going to enjoy every second of it.

"We can," I murmur, trying to kiss that lipstick off her. It ain't working. "But I'm not popping your cherry in the back of a bar, Addison."

"How do you know it's my first time?"

"You are itching for that spanking," I growl, pissed by the mere thought of her giving what's mine to someone else. "I can smell the virginity on you, baby girl."

She sniffs like she's trying to smell it. Just that quick, I'm smiling again.

I kiss her hard and then scowl. "Why ain't this shit coming off?"

"It's lip stain."

"Whatever it is, you look too beautiful in it," I mutter. "That dress too. Don't know how I'm supposed to keep my hands off you."

"Who said you had to try?" she asks, tipping her head back to meet my gaze. "I certainly don't remember setting that rule." Her smile is full of mischief and bad intentions, both of which have my cock leaking again. So does the way she ducks under my arm and sashays into the living room.

I spin to watch her, palming my cock through my jeans at the way her ass sways.

"You definitely want a spanking," I mutter, shaking my head. She picked that dress intentionally. I'm guessing every single thing she put in that bag was an intentional choice, made to remind me that she's all woman. I'm not going to stop her. Won't anyone else get close to her tonight because she won't be leaving my sight and our group will have the place to ourselves.

Her quiet laughter floats toward me. God, how did I go seven months without her speaking to me? Without making her laugh? Never again.

"I like you talking," I say, striding across the room toward her to slide an arm around her waist. I press a kiss to her temple before heading toward the elevator. "Didn't think I'd ever win you over enough to get you talking to me."

"I didn't want to embarrass myself," she says, her voice small. She hides her eyes from me, glancing down at her feet. "I, um...I have trouble talking to people sometimes."

"You're shy."

"A little bit. Mostly, I'm just anxious."

I hit the button for the floor below us and then bustle her onto the elevator. We're not actually leaving the hotel. Bentley rented out one of the rooftop bars for us. Easiest way to go out without causing a scene or being bombarded by fans wanting photos.

"You were anxious to talk to me?" I ask once we're on the elevator.

Addison peeks up at me, her expression full of worry. "Promise you won't laugh?"

"I'd never laugh at you or make fun of you. Anyone who does isn't worthy of you." I stroke her jawline, trying to soothe her.

"I used to have a stutter," she whispers. "Sometimes, when I meet new people or get really nervous, I still stutter. Um, people used to make fun of me for it a lot. I was so afraid I would try to say something to you and would start stuttering and you'd laugh too."

"Little one," I say, my heart breaking. She's stuttered before. She's done it several times today. I probably should have put two and two together, but I didn't. My poor little angel. How could anyone make fun of her for anything, let alone for something out of her control? I want to find everyone who did and put my boot up their asses.

I pull her into my arms to hold her instead.

"I'm sorry you went through that," I say, my lips against her crown. "I hate that assholes made you afraid to use your own voice. You have the sweetest voice. Even when you stutter, baby."

"It wasn't just them. I ran off and got lost in the woods one night when I was little," she mumbles, hiding her face in my throat. "A farmer found me the next morning, but I couldn't even tell him my name. And then the news people kept trying to get me to talk. I guess it gave me a complex."

"Assholes," I growl, wishing like hell I'd been there to protect her from that. Reporters can be difficult. They have no concept of personal boundaries. Far too often, I've had them follow me around, shoving microphones and cameras in my face. That they did it to a traumatized little girl pisses me off, but it doesn't surprise me.

That won't be happening again.

I'll hire whoever I need to hire to make sure no one gets close to her. She's mine to protect now, and I won't let anyone make her afraid to use her own voice. Forget that.

"You don't have to talk to anyone you don't want to talk to," I promise her as the elevator stops. "Including me. If you don't feel like talking, you just come curl up on my lap and I'll hold you until you can't even remember why you were afraid."

The doors of the elevator open, so I pull her out into the hallway and then hit the button for the public elevator so we can go back to the top floor.

She lifts her head to look at me, her lips slightly parted. "I like talking to you."

"Yeah?"

She nods. "I don't feel afraid with you anymore. Not since...."

"Not since I made you feel like you didn't have a choice," I finish for her, my stomach sinking like a stone. I knew it took a hell of a lot for her to speak up for herself yesterday, but I didn't realize just how much courage it really took. I know different now. My girl isn't just shy. She's literally afraid to speak. Realizing that makes me feel about two inches tall. "I'm so damn sorry, Addison. What I said yesterday was fucked up and it wasn't true. You couldn't ever be in the way. Getting to spend time with you could never be anything less than the best gift I've ever got."

"Why did you say it?" she asks. She isn't judging me though, and she isn't mad. I think she's genuinely curious.

"Thought someone should try to save you from me," I mutter, telling her the truth. "Ain't nothing sweet about the way I want you, baby. I'm a rough, dirty bastard. Knew if they sent you here with me, there wouldn't be any staying away from you."

"I don't want to stay away from you," she whispers.

"Good because that shit ended the minute you said you were coming with me. I've tried like hell to convince myself to stay away and let you find yourself a good man, one who deserves you. I ain't trying anymore."

"What if I think you are the man who deserves me?" she asks, her eyes flitting from mine to my lips, back and forth so fast I know what she's after, what she's thinking. And I want to give it to her, show her all those things she wants me to teach her, but not yet.

I promised her a date, and that's what she's getting.

"Then I'll spend every minute of the day thanking God," I murmur. "And just as many trying to be worthy of you. I reckon I'll fuck it up along the way, but if you want me, I'm yours, Addison. Have been since day one."

"You're all I've ever wanted," she whispers, so much longing in her voice it makes my knees weak. "It's crazy to me to think you could feel the same way. I'm just me. And you're you."

"I'm just a man."

"No," she says, shaking her head. "You're one of the best men I've ever met. Even though you're this big star, you still treat me like I matter. You treat everyone that way. You're never mean or rude. You don't pretend I don't exist. Even when I didn't talk to you, you brought me coffee and you sent me the most beautiful flowers for my birthday."

"You knew they were from me?"

"You're the only person who calls me little one."

"You are little," I murmur, which is true. When I wrap my hands around her waist, my fingers nearly touch. Maybe it's wrong how much I love how tiny she is, but I do love it. I can wrap her up in me and keep her safe. "You're this cuddly little thing with the bluest eyes and biggest smile. Ain't never met anyone who lights up a room like you do."

The elevator finally arrives. I help her on and then press the button for the top floor.

"Why are we going back upstairs?" she asks, looking at me like I've lost my mind.

"You'll see."

She eyes me for a minute and then seems to decide it doesn't matter and shrugs.

"Shit."

"What?"

"It's a karaoke bar," I mutter, worried going will make her anxious or make her feel like she has to get up and sing. "It'll just be us, Bentley, Cami, Kasen, and Olivia, and the staff, but you don't have to sing. You don't have to do anything you don't want to do."

"Okay," she whispers, chewing on her bottom lip.

I reach out and run my fingertip over it. "You keep that up, you'll hurt yourself."

"Sorry. Nervous habit."

"Don't be nervous," I murmur, pulling her back into my arms. "I'll be right here with you. No one will judge you or think badly of you if you don't get up on stage. Cami and Olivia love you. Kasen and Bentley do too."

That makes her giggle. "You sound so mad about it."

"I'm possessive as hell when it comes to you," I admit. "You talking to Kasen but not to me about drove me insane with jealousy."

"He's easy to talk to," she says softly. "He's crazy."

"Ain't that the truth," I mutter, which makes her laugh again. The man's crazier than an outhouse rat. Actually kidnapped his girl until she agreed to marry him. Hell, maybe I'm crazy too. The thought of kidnapping Addison until she's got my ring on her finger and my baby in her belly is mighty tempting.

If she didn't have school, I might actually do it. But I ain't coming between her and her education. She's too smart. I won't ever be the thing that keeps her from getting her degree and smashing every goal she set for herself. If she wants to be President, I'll be First Man and won't be sorry about it. Whatever she wants.

"What do you want to do when you graduate?"

"I'm doing dual degrees in art and music studies," she says. "I'm kind of hoping Riley will keep me on. I love what I'm doing for all of you. If not, I would love to do album artwork."

I make a mental note to ask Riley to let her do the artwork for my next album. Don't even need to see her ideas. She's a hell of a photographer and has an eye for details. The graphics she puts together for Riley always look fantastic.

"You're talented, baby."

"Thanks." She gives me another one of those big smiles that knocks me on my ass.

The elevator arrives on the top floor.

"Oh, wow," she whispers when the doors slide open to a view of Chattanooga laid out below us, lights shining like a million stars. Fire pits and plush, hardy furniture are arranged in groupings all around the outdoor bar, with strands of lights giving it a warm glow. Even with the fire pits, the wind is frigid. One day, I'll bring her back here when it's warm. For tonight, we're indoors.

"Come on," I murmur, taking her hand to lead her toward the door that opens into the karaoke bar. The walls are all glass. Like the bar outside, comfortable furniture is arranged in groups, offering patrons privacy and comfort. A small, raised stage occupies one corner, with the bar running the length of the back wall.

We're the first ones here.

The bartender spots us and circles the bar, headed in our direction. She's maybe twenty-five, with blonde hair pulled up in a bun and a pair of purple glasses. She's tall and curvy. Her gaze runs over both of us before she smiles.

"Looks like y'all are the first to arrive," she says, stopping in front of us and holding out her hand. "I'm Jessa. I'll be serving you tonight."

"I'm Clayton," I murmur, shaking her hand. "This is my girlfriend, Addison."

Addison startles beside me.

"Hi," she whispers to Jessa.

"Your dress is gorgeous," Jessa says, smiling at her. She's friendly, genuine. "You look incredible. If y'all want to pick a seat, I'll bring you menus. The place is yours tonight so you can sit wherever you like. I can whip you up something while you wait for everyone else. You know what you want to drink?"

"What do you want, little one?" I murmur to Addison.

"Um...can I just have water?" she asks, her voice whisper quiet.

"Water for her, and I'll have a beer. Something local," I tell Jessa.

"I'll bring it right out." She smiles again and then heads back to the bar area.

I lead Addison over to a table to the right of the stage. A set of couches are grouped beside it in case we want to get more comfortable after we eat. I help her into a chair and then press my lips to her shoulder, unable to resist. Her skin is soft.

She shivers, her skin pebbling.

"Love the way your body responds to me," I mutter, claiming the seat beside her. I hook my foot around the bottom of her chair and pull it closer to mine so I can wrap an arm around her. Touching her is addictive.

"You s-s-s-said girlfriend."

"Hmm?"

"You c-called me your g-girlfriend." Her blue eyes are wide with shock.

"What would you call us?" I ask, not sure there is a word that describes what this beautiful woman is to me. She's my one, the only person on this planet that carries a piece of my soul in her. The only one to lay claim to every square inch of my heart. I don't know what word describes that, but I do know she's the one person who could have talked sense into me back when I needed to hear it.

For a chance with her, there's not much I wouldn't do. Walking away from the club—hell, not getting sucked into that shit in the first place—wouldn't have required a single moment of thought had I known she existed back then. I can't go back and redo it. Maybe getting involved in all that shit is what led me to her to begin with. I don't know, but she's mine and I'll proudly wear whatever label she wants to put on us until I've got my ring on her finger.

I've never had a girlfriend, never been in a serious relationship. Hell, I ain't even got my dick wet since I got out of prison. Hopping from bed to bed or sharing women with my brothers in the club never interested me before then. Once I got out, I had other things to occupy my time, like buying back my dad's bar. As a felon, that shit wasn't easy. Riley and Cash showed up not even a year after I accomplished it. Still own the bar even if I no longer run it.

"I don't know what to call us." Her face scrunches up like it does when she's thinking about something, trying to sort it out for herself.

"I'll be calling you my wife soon," I murmur, lifting her hand to my lips to brush a kiss across her knuckles. "Just as soon as you decide to let me."

Her eyes go comically wide and her mouth drops open.

She's so fucking cute, all wide-eyed and shocked, looking at me like I just shook the foundation of her world. Shouldn't be legal to be so damn beautiful.

"You don't drink?" I ask, putting a finger beneath her chin to close her mouth.

She blinks and then shakes her head like she's trying to clear it. "You're crazy."

"Nah, baby girl. I've been crazy for the last seven months," I murmur, flipping her hand over to kiss her palm. And then I nip the side of her wrist. She's edible from head to toe. Ain't a single part of her that doesn't taste like sunshine and sugar. "I'm right as rain now that you're in my arms."

"I'm not old enough."

"To marry me? The hell you ain't," I growl. "When I put a baby in your belly, you'll be wearing my ring on your finger, Addison." Don't care which comes first, they're both happening, sooner rather than later. She's been mine for less than a day and I'll already fight hammer to tongs to keep her, even if I have to take a page from Kasen's book and kidnap her to convince her to marry me.

She stares at me for a minute and then her expression goes soft and she laughs. "To drink, Clayton. I'm not old enough to drink."

Well, hell.

"Seems to me, if you're old enough to wear that pretty dress and grind all over my cock, you ought to be old enough to have a beer if you want one," I mutter. If she wants to drink, I want it to be while I'm here to watch out for her.

The rules don't apply when you make as much money as I do. People look the other way, pretend not to see all kinds of shit when they're looking at money. They can damn sure look the other way if my girl wants a beer.

"I've never had beer before," she admits, still smiling at me like I'm her hero.

"Never?"

"Nope. Just wine. Laney and I tried whiskey once." She scrunches up her face and shudders, making it clear what she thinks about whiskey. "It was horrible!"

"It wasn't good whiskey then."

"Is there a difference?"

"Is there a...?" I gape at her, which makes her giggle again. "You grew up in Tennessee and you're asking me if there's a difference in whiskey? Baby, you're getting a good ole' country education tonight."

Chapter Seven

Addison

"**S**hake it, baby!" Olivia shouts at Kasen, who is on stage with Bentley and Clayton.

He winks at her and then does a little jig.

Cami and I collapse in a fit of giggles.

Bentley and Clayton just shake their heads at us. Like Olivia, Bentley isn't drinking tonight. Olivia is pregnant, so she can't. I think Bentley is staying sober to keep an eye on the rest of us. Clayton hasn't been drinking much either. I've had two glasses of wine and a few sips of whatever Cami is drinking. It's going to my head.

I'm not drunk, but my lips are tingling, and I feel completely relaxed.

Clayton let me try whiskey. I'm still not impressed, but I'm not going to tell him that. I think he finds it personally offensive that I don't like whiskey. It's not my fault though. It tastes like a hangover if a hangover had a taste. I may not be old enough to drink legally, but I've had a few of those. Laney and I have wine and movie nights. Well, we did before she got married.

Tonight has been so much fun. Clayton has been all over me, so Kasen and Bentley have been giving him hell. He just flips them off and goes back to whispering sweet things in my ear. I've never seen him so happy and relaxed, like he doesn't have a care in the world.

Cami noticed it too. When the guys got up to sing, she leaned over and told me that we both look so happy. It's not the alcohol that has me floating miles above the ground. It's Clayton. Yesterday, I thought my heart was going to rip itself into tiny pieces. Today, I think it's going to swell so big it explodes.

He thinks he doesn't deserve me. I don't think anyone has ever been more deserving than he is. He may have done things in his past that were wrong, but he's a genuinely good man, trying to make amends and redeem himself. I still don't understand exactly what he did, but I do know that he regrets it, that he thinks I should be ashamed of him. I'm not. I could never look at him and feel shame. I love him, and I'm falling deeper by the minute.

"Oh, I love this song," Olivia says as the first few bars of *Tennessee Whiskey* flow from the speakers.

"This one is for you, baby girl," Clayton says, pointing at me. "You boys ready to give her that ole' country education?"

"Let's do the damn thing," Bentley says.

"Yeehaw!" Kasen shouts.

Even Jessa, who is hanging out near the bar, laughs at him.

We stop laughing as soon as Clayton sings the first line. Jesus. His voice is incredible. I think he could sing a grocery list and sound amazing, but this song in particular was made for a voice like his. He sounds so good.

When Kasen and Bentley join in on the chorus, it gets even better. I've heard them sing a million times. But I have never heard the three of them sing together before now.

Holy crap. They're good.

"Holy crap," Cami whispers, echoing my thoughts.

I glance over at Olivia to find her staring at the three of them in shock.

Bentley and Clayton both have deep, soulful baritones that shine on the lower notes, and Kasen is able to hit the higher notes with crazy precision. They sound phenomenal together, definitely not like any karaoke I've ever heard before now.

"If they don't cover this song together, it'll be a tragedy," Olivia says.

"No kidding," Cami mutters, pulling out her phone. She messes with it for a second and then holds it up, recording them.

I pull mine out to take a couple pictures of them. I should have brought my camera but it's in my bag downstairs. They look like they're having a blast up there. Clayton is at home on stage in a way he isn't anywhere else. When he has his guitar in his hands or a microphone in front of him, he's pure sex.

There's a reason why women go crazy for him, and it's not just because he's gorgeous. It's the way he moves and the way he sounds and that little boy grin. He has a way of singing that makes you feel like he's singing just for you. It's captivating.

Kasen hops down from the stage and prowls toward Olivia, which makes her giggle and shoo him away. He just shakes his head and holds out a hand for her. She gives up and rolls her eyes, taking his hand. Once she's on her feet, he wraps one arm around her and sways, crooning the lyrics in her ear.

"Aww," Cami says, turning to capture them on video.

I turn back to the stage to see Clayton staring at me. My eyes lock with his, my entire body tingling at the intense look on his face. God, he's so beautiful. He makes me feel that way too, like I'm the most beautiful thing he's ever seen.

He took his sunglasses off this morning and hasn't put them back on since. Every time I look up, he's looking at me. And not in a way that's accidental. His eyes are full of passion, of purpose, like he's staring at me intentionally, not because he can't control it, but because there's nothing else in the world he'd rather look at. He has a million different places he could look, but he chooses to look at me. All the time.

Nothing has ever made me feel as confident as that realization does. For the first time in my life, I don't feel like the anxious, timid little girl who can't speak and has to sleep with the light on. I don't feel embarrassed or out of place. I feel like a woman, powerful, sexy, and confident. This is where I'm supposed to be, right here with Clayton.

"I want to sing."

Cami turns to me in shock.

My heart thuds against my ribcage, but I don't let it scare me into silence.

Not this time. Not tonight.

"I want to sing," I repeat. My whole life, music has given me comfort, but I've never sang in front of anyone. The slumber party that ended in disaster is the first, and last, time I shared my voice with anyone. I may not be superstar good, but I can sing.

"You're sure?" Cami asks.

I bob my head, decisive. I need to do this. More than that, I *want* to do this. Not because I have anything to prove to anyone, but because this is one of those moments I want to be able to look back on in twenty years and not regret a single second of it. It's one of those rare, perfect moments we all have that get us through the hard times and the ugly times and the times when nothing is going right. Life is made up of those moments, sprinkled between the everyday, ordinary stuff and the hard stuff like little presents from the universe to let us know we're doing all right.

This is one of those moments, I'm sure of it.

Cami scrutinizes my expression and then waves Jessa over.

"What's up?" Jessa asks.

"Addison wants to go next," Olivia tells her as Kasen hops back up onstage.

"What song do you want?" Jessa asks, turning to me with a smile. I really like her. She's been incredibly nice to us all night, and not in a flirty way either. She's been respectful and friendly and hasn't made the guys feel uncomfortable even once.

I lean up to whisper my choice to her.

"Oh, nice," she says. "I'll queue it up after they finish."

"Thank you."

I glance back up at the stage to see Clayton staring at me still. His lips quirk up into that grin I love so much. I smile back, my heart fluttering.

"He's so good for you," Cami leans over to whisper to me. "I've never seen you so happy."

"I don't think I've ever been this happy," I whisper back, my eyes still locked on Clayton. He isn't just good for me. He's good *to* me. And I know, even if I get up there and freeze up, no one here will judge me or laugh at me. I won't regret it. But I will always regret not trying.

Clayton holds my gaze as they finish the song. The heat in his eyes makes me shiver. I want to feel him pressed to me again, want to feel him on top of me. He says he's rough and dirty as if he's ashamed of the way he wants me. But God, I want him like that so bad it actually hurts.

To be the reason he unravels, the reason he trembles...I've never wanted anything as badly as I want to be the one to bring him to his knees. And I don't want to do it to prove that I'm a woman—I know he sees me that way now. I want to do it just because I can. Just because I want every piece of him, and I want him to have every piece of me.

"Bravo!" Olivia cheers when the song ends.

Cami and I both clap and whistle too.

Kasen bows like this was a performance instead of karaoke...which it might as well have been. Karaoke with superstars is a stacked racket no one else could hope to win. Luckily, this isn't a competition. The guys are just having fun, singing for themselves instead of for a packed house for once. They get to be themselves and do what they love with no pressure.

Clayton hops off the stage and stalks toward me.

"Chris Stapleton is in trouble," I murmur, smiling up at him. "You just owned that song."

"Yeah?" He leans down to kiss me. Whiskey tastes far better on his lips than it does in his glass. "You change your mind about whiskey yet?"

"The song is great. The drink still sucks!" Olivia whisper-shouts.

I laugh against Clayton's lips.

"Who did I even marry?" Kasen asks, sounding horrified.

"A goddess," Olivia says.

"Damn right."

Clayton and I both laugh this time. He kisses me again and then lets me go, reclaiming his seat beside me on the couch. We all moved to the couches after we ate.

"If you guys don't record that song, Riley is killing all of you," Cami says. "I'm helping."

"Same," Olivia chimes in.

"Me too."

The guys look at each other and then shrug.

"I'm in," Kasen says.

"I'll do it for kisses," Bentley mutters to Cami, who promptly leans over and kisses him.

"You really want us to record it, baby girl?" Clayton asks, trailing a hand down my shoulder.

"Um, yes! Are you kidding me? That was amazing," I say. "I don't know how I'm supposed to top that."

Clayton pulls back to look at me, a question in his eyes.

"I want to sing."

"You don't have to sing, little one," he murmurs. "No one will be mad."

"I want to do it," I promise him. My stomach flutters with nerves, but it's not the same as when I freeze up. When that happens, my heart races and my entire body gets hot and then cold. The flutters are so big they grip my whole body and I start shaking. These are little flutters, the normal kind.

He scrutinizes my expression just like Cami did, looking for any hint that I don't want to do this. Whatever he sees there seems to reassure him that I'm all right. He leans forward, touching his lips to mine before he presses them to my ear.

"Sing for me then, little one. Let me hear how sweet you're going to sound when I'm inside you. Make my dick hard enough to hurt," he whispers in my ear before pulling the lobe into his mouth to bite it.

"Clayton," I whimper, gripping onto the cushion to keep myself upright as a wave of heat blasts through me, blowing hot enough to send my body temperature soaring.

"Go sing your song," he says, giving me a sweet kiss on the cheek and then rising to his feet. He holds a hand out to me.

I spy his glass of whiskey on the table and take a drink of it, only to cough and splutter as it burns its way down. It's so awful. I don't care what they say, whiskey is not good. As soon as it hits my stomach, I feel the warmth spreading.

"Gah!" I say, shuddering.

"We're revoking your membership to the cool kids' club," Kasen says, laughing at me.

"Take mine too," Olivia sasses. "Whiskey sucks."

"You know what else su...ow!" Kasen says, spluttering and laughing when Olivia kicks him in the shin, glaring at him. "I wasn't going to say anything bad."

"Mmhmm."

Clayton helps pull me to my feet while Olivia and Kasen bicker. I think he says crazy things just to rile her up so he can kiss her happy again. He does it a lot, and he always smiles the whole time.

"Whoa, baby. Steady," Clayton murmurs when I stumble.

It's not the alcohol though. It's the man. He made my legs all shaky.

"I think you're done for the night. Don't want you getting sick on me."

"I'm okay," I promise, even though I don't plan on drinking anything else.

I let him lead me to the stage and help me climb the stairs. He frowns like he's worried I'm going to fall off, but

I really am okay. I have a little buzz, but I'm not drunk. He just has a habit of making me weak in the knees.

I position myself in front of the monitor in case I need the lyrics and then grab the microphone. My stomach flutters again, a little more forcefully this time. Being brave was a lot easier when I was sitting on the couch. It's harder when I'm standing on the stage and everyone is looking at me.

"You don't have to do this," Clayton murmurs, positioning himself in front of me to block everyone else out. I see the worry in his eyes, hear it in his voice.

"I want to do this," I say. I haven't changed my mind. I'm just a little nervous. "Um, but will you stay up here with me? Please?"

"Wouldn't want to be anywhere else," he says, his lips tipping up into a sweet smile. "Sing your song so I can tell you how brave you are and try to kiss that lip stain off you."

I smile at that. He's been trying all night, complaining on and off that it won't come off. Which is kind of the point of using it. It has staying power.

"Exotic dancers used to use it on their nipples to make them more noticeable," I say.

"What the fuck?"

"That's what it was originally made for, but now we use it on our lips and cheeks."

"I..." He opens his mouth and then closes again and shakes his head. "I ain't even going to ask how you know that. Sing your song, Addison."

I take a deep breath and then nod and reach for the microphone.

"You can do this, brave girl," he murmurs to me, reaching for my free hand.

I clutch onto him gratefully, squeezing his hand. My heart pounds against my ribcage, but I still don't feel frozen. I close my eyes and take another deep breath, trying to imagine myself at home in my room like my speech therapist used to tell me to do.

The music starts, the first strains of *Black Velvet* spilling from the speakers.

Everyone at the table gets quiet.

"It's just me and you, little one," Clayton murmurs, squeezing my hand.

I let out a shaky breath, nod, and then start to hum.

"Oh, shit," Kasen whispers.

"Mississippi in the middle of a dry spell," I sing. My voice shakes on the first word before leveling out. I lose myself in the first verse, swaying to the beat.

Clayton is completely still in front of me.

The whole room is quiet.

I crack my eyes open to see Clayton staring at me like he wants to tumble me to the floor and do dirty things to me. Seeing him looking at me like that makes me feel powerful all over again. My voice gains strength, my confidence growing.

I sing to him, blocking out the rest of the room. He's the reason I picked this song. Clayton is gruff and dark where Elvis was smooth and charming. But he has that same magnetism and sex appeal that you can't help but notice.

He's staring at me like he's a big cat preparing to pounce. His eyes are so dark, they're almost black with lust. His chest rises and falls, his breath rasping in his throat. He's breaking. I see the cracks growing bigger in front of my eyes. I want to tip him over the edge.

I release his hand and spin around, backing up against him. He slides his arm around my waist, splaying his hand against my abdomen like he did in the suite at lunch. This time, I raise my free arm and wrap it around his neck, securing myself to his body as I sway and grind against him, belting out the song from memory.

I feel the growl vibrating in his chest and his breath hitting my neck as those cracks grow bigger. So does his erection, until I feel it pressed against my bottom, nestling between my cheeks. I sway my hips and shimmy.

He growls again, the sound feral.

God, I love that sound. Love the way he feels up against me, all hot and hard and trembling with desire. Every time he touches me, I ache. Every time he kisses me, I catch fire and burn. But he's been in control every time, stopping us before we could get too far. Not this time. His control is in tatters around him. He's burning too, blazing hot as the sun. I did this to him, made him exactly as crazy as he's been making me all day long.

I hum the outro as the song ends.

"Holy shit. Addison can sing," Kasen says into the charged silence.

Everyone at the table starts clapping and cheering for me.

I barely hear them. All I can hear is Clayton. He doesn't let me go. He's breathing hard, shaking, his palm flat against my belly. I slowly slide my arm down, my fingertips trailing across his neck. He makes a sound that's somewhere between a groan and a growl. I feel it in my core.

"Thank you," I whisper to him.

He cracks.

I squeak as he spins me to face him, causing me to crash into his chest. The next thing I see is his eyes, blazing with heat before his mouth crashes down on mine. He kisses me hard, slipping his tongue in my mouth to set my veins on fire. They catch with a *whoosh* of sound, incinerating me.

I kiss him back just as desperately, unable to stop myself. His facial hair tickles at my jaw in a way that makes me want him more, need him more.

"Clayton," I gasp, my hands clenching and unclenching on his shirt.

He growls and tears himself away from me.

I whimper, but he's back before I can even miss him.

He swings me up into his arms, securing me against his body.

"We're leaving," he growls over his shoulder...to the group, I guess.

I hear them laughing and catcalling, but it sounds like it's coming from a distance. All my attention is focused on the man still trembling around me. He's everywhere, eclipsing everything else. I press my face into his throat, breathing him in. The ache grows, consuming every inch of my body. Everything hurts for him.

"Clayton," I whimper.

"Hang on, little one," he growls.

I do, clinging to him like my life depends on it.

Right now, I think it might because if I let him go, it's going to kill me. I'm sure of it.

Chapter Eight

Clayton

Getting Addison back to the suite without fucking her up against a wall takes every bit of self-control I possess. I knew she was going to ruin me, but I didn't expect it'd happen on a karaoke stage while she sang like a goddess. By the time the elevator carries us down so we can swap to the private elevator, what little control I have left is in tatters.

My girl may be afraid to use her voice, but I've never heard anything like her.

I expected her to sound like the angel she is. I did not expect her to completely nail a song most can't touch. She shocked the hell out of me and I ain't ashamed to admit it. Her voice is powerful, sexy without even trying. She is so damn brave, more than she realizes. The fact that she faced her fear to sing for me...God, I don't deserve her, but she's mine anyway.

"Clayton," she whimpers into my throat. She's trembling in my arms, shaking like a leaf.

"I know," I growl, trying to get my keycard out of my pocket to access the private elevator. Jesus. My dick gets any harder, I really will be fucking her up against a wall for her first time.

Addison grows impatient and nips my throat.

I growl, yanking the keycard free of my pocket, when she touches her tongue to that same spot. Somehow, I manage to insert the key card. The elevator doors slide open.

I stomp inside and hit the button for the suite. As soon as the doors close, I have her pressed against the wall, holding her captive with my body. Her legs encircle my waist, her right thigh exposed all the way to her hip because of the slit in her dress.

Our mouths meet, both of us desperate.

I drown myself in her, licking into her mouth to consume her. My hands run all over her, the need to claim her beating at me with every frenetic thump of my heart.

She plunges her hands into my hair, pulling.

"Shit," I growl, my body aching as the pain sends pleasure spiking higher. It feels like heaven. All my life, I've been big, a tough son of a bitch with the rap sheet to prove it. Yet somehow, this sweet little thing manages to wreck me with a single touch, turns me into a beast I don't even recognize. One so fucking hard up, I'm ready to beg.

The elevator dings, the doors sliding open. I rip my mouth from Addison's long enough to carry her inside. She put all her stuff in the smaller bedroom today, no doubt thinking she would be sleeping there. She won't. When she falls asleep tonight, it'll be in my arms.

I carry her into the bigger bedroom, kicking the door closed behind us. The blinds are open, the moon shining brightly overhead. Can't see the stars because of all the light pollution, but the lights of the city shine like diamonds, illuminating the dips and thrusts of the mountains in the distance.

I drop Addison on the bed.

She cries out, her sweet voice full of disappointment. It don't last long. I refuse to let it. My girl needs to come, and I'm going to make her. When I get inside her, she'll be stone-cold sober. But I can take care of her.

I pull her heels off her feet, kissing the top of each foot. Her toes are topped with sparkly pink polish. Her feet are as tiny as the rest of her and just as soft. I press my lips to the delicate bone of her ankle, kissing a trail up to her knee. Her skin feels like fine silk beneath my lips. She really is edible from head to toe.

Ripping her pretty dress should probably make me feel bad. It don't. The thing is standing between me and heaven. Hell itself couldn't keep me from debauching this girl. A dress damn sure ain't going to do it.

She moans when I grab hold of the fabric at the split in the thigh. It doesn't take much effort to tear it. The fabric shreds all the way up to her belly. My cock throbs at the sight of her panties. They're virgin white lace with a red ribbon-like bow along the waistband. Like her dress, they're indecently sexy.

"Going to wreck this thing when I get in it," I growl, staring at her pussy like it's the holy grail. I think it might be. It's barely big enough to take my pinky, let alone my cock. The lace clings to the lips of her pussy where her cream soaked them through. Her cunt is bare.

Her stomach quivers and she moans like she's completely on board with that plan.

I gotta see the rest of her. I've been dreaming about this damn near nightly since the day I met her. Jerked my cock raw thinking about those tits, trying to imagine the exact shade of her nipples and how hard they'd be for me. Ain't a whole lot on her I didn't think about while fucking my hand.

"Clayton," she whimpers, chafing her thighs together when I rip the dress again, clean up the middle.

"You aren't wearing a bra," I growl as soon as those little tits spring free, jiggling in my face. They're the biggest part of her body. Her nipples are hard pebbles topping those gorgeous mounds in the prettiest shade of pink. My imagination didn't do her justice, didn't come close to it.

"C-couldn't with my dress," she says, her voice thick with desire, heavy with need.

I quickly strip her dress the rest of the way off her, breaking the string that ties up around her neck. The chains are part of the dress. They slither together, rustling as I toss the ruined fabric over the side of the bed and then sit back on my heels to look at her.

"Jesus Christ," I breathe, squeezing my dick like that's going to make me less likely to break my own rule and pop her cherry here and now. I'm hanging on by a thread already. Seeing her spread out against the black bedding is, by far, the sexiest thing I've ever seen.

It shouldn't be legal for her to look this good.

I fish my phone out of my pocket, needing to capture this image so I can pull it out and look at it over and over.

"W-what are you doing?" she whispers, her voice wary. Her tongue darts out, wetting her bottom lip.

"Taking a picture of the prettiest thing I've ever seen." I open my camera app and snap several photos of her.

"W-what if s-s-someone s-sees?"

"I'd never let that happen, little one," I murmur, meeting her gaze. The mere thought of anyone else seeing her like this, all ruffled and pink and turned on has fury churning through me. No one sees her like this except me. "Going to be jacking my cock raw to these while you're in class and working."

She swallows hard, her pupils dilating.

"You like knowing how hot you make me, don't you?"

She nods, licking her lips again. "I l-like it," she whispers. "It makes me feel..."

"Sexy? You're definitely that, Addison. So sexy. Jesus, you got me shaking over you."

"No, powerful." Her eyes meet mine again, those baby blues wide and earnest...and excited. "I like knowing you enjoy looking at me."

"Enjoy it? Baby, I enjoy whiskey and playing my guitar. I live for looking at you. That sweet smile, those pretty blue eyes, that gorgeous body. Can't keep my eyes off you," I mutter. "Spent seven months coming up with reasons to go see Riley just so I could look at you. You got me addicted to you."

"Me too."

"Spread your legs. Let me see my pussy."

She chafes her thighs together, her stomach quivering again. She gives me what I want though, parting her thighs so I can take a picture of the way her panties cling to her lips. I snap a few and then toss my phone onto the nightstand, confident no one will ever see them but me.

"Jesus, baby, you're so pretty and pink here."

She cries out, arching upward as I press my thumb to the seam of her panties and jiggle it.

I prowl up her body, gliding my mouth up her thigh and then over her hip. She shivers as my beard tickles her skin. I nip at her belly right above her panties, growling when I smell her. She's sweet everywhere, like cotton candy and sex. I can't wait to eat her until she's creaming all over my tongue.

"Clayton," she whimpers, pulling my hair again when I capture one nipple in my mouth, playing with it. She writhes beneath me, rubbing against me in ways that ought to be criminal. If heaven is real, ain't no way it competes with this.

I bite her nipple, raking it through my teeth. She cries out my name, startled.

"I'm going to have so much fun with you and this body. Jesus, Addison. I don't even know where to start teaching you what you've been hurting for all day."

"Anywhere," she moans. "Clayton, please. I need you. Please."

There it is. The single best moment of my life. Her whining and begging, pleading for me because she knows I can give her what she needs, knows I'll take care of her. There ain't a whole lot in life that I can't live without. Hearing her say my name like that is at the top of the list.

"You sound so sweet when you're begging me, little one. You have any idea what I want to do to you?" I tongue her other nipple and then smack it just to see her tits jiggle again. Just because she's mine and I can. Just because I know her better than she does, know what she needs. She may be an angel, but she's a woman too. And I'm the lucky motherfucker who gets to teach her just how good she can feel.

"Clayton!" she cries out, trembling.

I smack her breast again, growling when she says my name like that again. Ain't a sweeter sound to be heard, not on this planet or any other. My self-control is already in tatters, but I can't stop playing with her tits. She's so responsive. Every time I kiss or bite, she whines. She isn't afraid to use her voice when I'm gorging myself on her tits, leaving my marks on her.

My cock is so hard it hurts. It's a hell of a thing though, being so hard yet not ever wanting to stop what I'm doing to her. Every time she says my name, my dick throbs. Every time I leave another mark on those gorgeous tits, it throbs again.

I kiss my way down her body, learning every dip and curve. She sobs when I nip at her belly. Trembles when I brush my lips across her ribcage. She pulls my hair again when I sink my teeth into her inner thigh, marking her there.

I flip her over onto her stomach to worship her this way too. The point where her shoulders meet her neck is sensitive. So are those little dimples above her ass.

"Clayton," she says, shocked when I yank her panties halfway down her thighs so I can kiss those supple cheeks. They're firm little buns, taunting me.

I sink my teeth into her right cheek. Spank her left.

She shouts when I spread them apart and bury my face between them. Her body tenses for a second before she melts into the bed, purring. I touch my tongue to her asshole, jiggling it there.

She shouts again, shocked.

"This is mine, Addison," I growl. "I'll eat it when I want, fuck it how I want."

"Oh my God."

I spank her again and then bury my face between her cheeks a second time. I can taste her cream where it's dripped down the crevice of her ass. I lick it all up, only for her to drip more. She may be shocked to have me playing with that little hole, but she loves it.

I flip her onto her back again, desperate to get my mouth on her pussy. She doesn't resist me at all, just lets me move her where I want, how I want. The fact that she trusts me with her body is a hell of a drug.

I slide her panties down her legs and then shove them in the pocket of my jeans. She won't be getting them back. They smell like her. I'll be fucking myself raw with them while I look at the pictures I took.

"My God. Look at this little thing," I growl, wedging myself between her legs. Her lower lips are spread open, revealing her folds. She's slick with her juices and as pretty pink here as she is everywhere else. Her clit is hard and swollen, practically begging for attention. I want to own every inch of that cunt, make her scream. My name will be the only one she ever screams. When I'm done with her, it'll be the only one she remembers.

"Clayton, it hurts," she whispers. She's writhing on top of the bed, her eyes so dilated her irises look like little more than thin blue rings around her pupils. She's so turned on she's shaking, her teeth chattering.

"Poor little angel," I croon, getting comfortable between her legs so I can take care of her. Leaving her hurting is hurting me. She shouldn't ever be anything less than perfectly happy. I press my nose to the juncture of her thigh and inhale deeply. Her smell sends a bolt of lust ripping through me.

I grasp her thighs and yank her closer to me, brush my nose through her folds. It nudges against her clit, which makes her cry out.

"Clayton, please!" she sobs, digging her nails into my hands. "Please. It hurts."

I spread her cheeks and lift her toward my mouth. Her cotton candy taste hits my system, blowing through my defenses like a hurricane. The sound that leaves my lips isn't one I've made before. It's a triumphant roar and a broken sob at the same time.

I don't take my time with her. I can't. I lick from her clit to her ass, lapping up her juices like a dog. My tongue circles her clit before I dip lower, trying to fuck her with it. She's tight as hell, resisting even that small intrusion.

That's all right though. I got all night.

I give up on getting my tongue in that hole for the moment and press it to the tight rim of her ass. She bucks beneath me, going wild for me. I have to let go of her ass and put my arm across her abdomen to hold her down so she's exactly where I want her.

Addison has always been so calm and quiet. Nothing much riles her or gets her worked up. Me eating her does the trick. She's hot for it, sobbing in pleasure and babbling my name. I run my tongue in circles around her clit again before moving back to her hole.

This time, I manage to get the tip of it inside her. I fuck her with it, show her what it's going to be like when I finally get inside her. She thinks I'm sweet. She'll learn. I've been desperate for her for so long, all that's left is the primal instinct to fuck and claim and own, to possess her as thoroughly as she does me.

I replace my tongue with my finger, fighting like hell to get inside her. Laying the flat of my tongue against her clit and rapidly flicking that little nub loosens her up enough for me to slip my finger inside her. I pump and twist and play, drowning in her.

Jesus God.

First time I felt my bike vibrating beneath my thighs, I thought I'd found heaven. I missed riding more than I missed anything else when I was locked up. Missed feeling the wind on my face and the sun beating down on me. Having my face buried between her legs while she's crying my name eclipses that joy by miles.

She's so close to coming all over my face. I feel her thighs trembling and her muscles clamping down on my finger, hear the hitch in her breath that grows more pronounced. I pull her clit into my mouth and suck hard, curling my finger up to stroke her g-spot at the same time.

She screams when she comes, wailing my name into the room like an aria.

My blood heats to boiling, flashes to steam.

I eat her through it, snarling savagely. Can't stop the sound. Can't stop eating her either. Her juices soak my mustache and beard, keeping her sweet smell all over me.

"Again," I growl, not letting up even when she falls limp beneath me. Filthy sounds fill the room, curses and grunts and the wet suck of my mouth against her pussy.

She claws at the bed like a wild thing, trying to wriggle away one minute and then pulling me closer the next. Her sobs of pleasure fill the room. It's the sweetest song I've ever heard, and it's all mine. She is mine, caught in the same net that ensnared me. I don't want it to let me go.

I live and breathe for this woman. I'm so in love with her. All I think about is her. All I want is her, always. Always.

Every second I spend with her just embeds her even deeper under my skin. She's an obsession, consuming me over and over again. It's light and dark, heaven and hell. And I don't ever want it to stop.

When she's right on the edge this time, I slip my pinky in her ass, playing with that pretty hole too. I shouldn't be doing any of this to a virgin, shouldn't be defiling her like this. I can't stop. Don't want to stop. If having my finger in her ass and my tongue in her pussy is what sentences me to hell, I'll burn happily.

She breaks for me, cracking right down the middle. My name rips from her lips in a way that's almost painful. Tears of ecstasy drip down her gorgeous face as her body locks up tight and then practically convulses. Her sweaty hair is plastered to her head and tangled all around her. She's wrecked, ruined, and I've never found her more beautiful.

As soon as she stops coming, I rear up over her, clawing at the fly of my jeans, trying to get them undone. I sob in relief when my cock springs free. I use her juices as lube, jerking myself off with her sticky cream all over my hand.

Four pumps and I'm shouting her name, roaring it into the room.

Her eyes flash open as the first thick rope of cum lands against her pussy and thighs. Those blue eyes hold me captive as I jerk off on her, covering her in my cum. She watches me intently, her pupils still dilated. She's dazed, but her tongue peeks out between her lips as if she wants to taste me there. The sight of it has my stomach clenching as another thick rope splashes against her belly.

I run my cock through her folds, biting down on my cheek to keep from crying out. Every nerve ending in my dick is sensitive. But the sight of me sliding through my own cum and her folds is the best damn thing I've ever seen.

"Clayton," she moans, letting me know she likes it too.

Jesus, this girl. Don't know where she came from or what I did to deserve her, but I'm keeping her. Even if doing it drags me right to hell. Spending a single lifetime with her is worth an eternity of torment. There's nothing I wouldn't endure to keep her looking at me this way, like I'm something special, some kind of beautiful she ain't ever seen before now.

I lean down and press my lips to her belly before collapsing beside her. I'm breathing hard, my side twinging like I just ran a foot race up a mountain. Somehow, I find the energy to pull her into my arms. She burrows in with the sweetest little sigh. You wouldn't ever know she was screaming my name not even five minutes ago.

"We didn't have sex," she says.

The pout in her voice makes me smile.

"You've been drinking, little one," I murmur, pressing a kiss to her sweaty forehead. "Ain't fucking you until you're sober enough to be sure I'm what you want. Once I get in you, it's permanent, Addison. There won't be any other man for you, not ever."

"Oh." She processes that for a moment. "Could you walk away now? If I said no?"

"You want the truth or the comforting lie?"

"The truth."

"I'd kill anyone who tried to take you from me now," I growl, meaning every word. She was mine seven months ago. She'll always be mine. Anyone tries to take her...well, I'm guessing prison won't feel much different a second time around.

"That should scare me, shouldn't it?"

"Does it?"

"No," she whispers. "I'm not afraid at all."

"Good. You never have to be afraid of me," I promise, my hand drifting through her tangled hair. "Knowing I hurt you yesterday damn near killed me. Won't be doing that shit again."

"I'm okay now." She presses a kiss to my jaw like she's trying to comfort me.

"Just okay? I ain't done something right then."

She giggles. "Better than okay. Amazing."

That's more like it.

Chapter Nine

I wake up with Clayton wrapped around me, placing sweet little kisses all over my neck. One of his hands cups my right breast. The other is between my legs, resting against my center.

"Wake up, little one," he croons, his chest vibrating against my back. He's like a giant heating blanket. I feel the heat of him even through his t-shirt.

Warmth spreads through me and I shiver. "I don't want to wake up," I murmur. "I'm having the best dream."

"Oh yeah?"

"Mmhmm. I'm naked in your bed."

"Open your eyes and you'll see it ain't a dream," he whispers. "You're definitely naked in our bed."

"I know. I'm in your arms and the whole world is perfect. I never want this dream to end," I whisper back.

"Then keep those eyes closed and I'll make it even better for you." He nudges my leg with his thigh, wedging it between mine to pry my legs open. He drapes the top one over his hip, opening me up to him. He's wearing boxers too, which really isn't fair. But I can feel his erection tenting the fabric, poking me in the back. His fingers drift along my sex.

"Clayton," I moan, remembering what he did to me last night. I've never felt anything like it. The things he said, the way he touched me...how he cleaned me up afterward. I barely remember that part. I was pretty out of it, drifting in and out of sleep.

"Mm," he hums, parting my folds with his finger. "I could listen to you saying my name like that forever and still never tire of it, little one."

"Clayton," I moan again, giving him what he wants.

He plays with my body like it belongs to him, like he knows exactly how to touch me to make me crazy. My heart thumps unevenly, my breath rasping in my throat. He shifts around behind me, and then I feel his erection between my legs. He's so hard...so damn big.

I slide my hand down my body before slipping it between my legs, eager to touch him like he's touching me. My hand slides along his shaft.

"Fuck," he growls, arching his hips into me, trying to get closer.

I'm so wet, embarrassingly so. He doesn't seem to mind. In fact, he seems to love how wet I am. Animalistic growls vibrate in his chest as we both explore. He's burning hot, somehow hard as steel and smooth as silk at the same time. I want him inside me.

I try to shift around to slip him inside, but he stops me.

"Not yet," he murmurs. "Like this." He rocks his hips so his erection slides back and forth through my folds, bumping against my clit every time.

I bite the pillow, trying to quiet my cries. It's no use. My whole body buzzes and hums like a million fireflies are trapped beneath my skin, dancing.

"Don't hide from me, Addison," he whispers. "Let me hear that pretty voice while you're soaking your man's cock with that sweet cream."

I release the pillow, unable to disobey the command in his voice. "Oh God."

"Who's making you feel good, little one?"

"Y-y-you are."

"Say my name," he growls. "Let the whole hotel know who this pussy belongs to, Addison."

"Clayton," I moan. And then louder, "Clayton."

"Good girl. Christ, I want to feel you choking on my cock while you're coming on my tongue," he groans, biting me.

The thought of taking him in my mouth has sweat breaking out all over my body. My womb clenches. I moan his name again, rocking my hips in time to his.

"God, yeah. Hump that little cunt all over my dick, baby girl," he growls, pinching my nipple. "It feels so fucking good. Ain't going to survive another night without claiming that cherry. It's mine. I want it."

"Yes, yes," I sob. "T-take it."

"Plan on it. Just as soon as I get you back to this room tonight."

"No, now," I demand, desperate for it. I won't survive until tonight. Already, I feel like I'm going to shatter into pieces if he isn't inside of me soon.

He smacks my pussy, making me cry out in shock, in pleasure. "I'm in charge here, Addison. I may let you play, but I decide when you come and how hard. I decide when to fuck you and how. You take what I give you."

"Clayton," I sob as he spanks me again and then again.

"Popping that cherry won't be something I fit in between breakfast and rehearsal," he growls in my ear. His beard and mustache tickle my skin, abrading it in a way that's far too appealing. They felt even better against my thighs when he was eating me last night. "I'm gonna take my sweet time with you, make you beg for it, Addison."

"Yes!" I cry, willing to give him anything so long as he doesn't stop what he's doing. My body is his to do with as he pleases. No one else could ever make me feel like this.

Like I'm soaring and falling at the same time. It feels so good. So good.

"Yeah, it does," he says, his voice whispering like sin. Only then do I realize I'm saying it out loud, chanting over and over that it feels so good.

He brings his hand down on me in a sharp smack. His name gets hung up in my throat, coming out as a wail as I shatter and break. Pleasure blasts through me like a fierce wind, molten in its intensity. The world splinters, cracking apart in a dizzying shower of color.

Clayton growls my name, and then I'm face down on the bed with his weight on top of me, pinning me to the mattress. He pumps his hips, grinding against my clit and snarling. His hand gets tangled in my hair, pulling my head back just hard enough to make it sting.

"Mine," he snarls against my lips, biting the bottom one. "This hot little cunt is mine."

His body locks up, his teeth sinking into my shoulder, making me cry out as another wave of pleasure blasts through me. And then he's coming. His seed spills across my bottom, splashing against my thighs.

Feeling him coming with his teeth in my skin while he's trembling and pinning me to the bed is enough to make my eyes roll back in my head. Nothing has ever felt as good as this. It's simply not possible.

This man...Lord, I don't know which of us is greedier, which of us is more obsessed. All I know is that he's mine and I'm his, and nothing in this world will ever change that.

I won't let it.

"Are you crazy?" I ask, gaping at Clayton from across the living room of our suite. "I can't have a spa day. I came here to work!"

"It's handled, little one. All that's left to do is run through our sets," he says, striding toward me. "We don't need you for that."

I narrow my eyes on him.

"It's handled," he says again, pulling me into his arms. "The stage is up; the band is here. Cami and Bentley met with the American Cancer Society rep and the hotel manager this morning. All you need to worry about today is finding you a dress."

"I have a dress."

"Not if I burn it," he growls, pulling me into his arms.

"You can't burn my dress! I need it for tonight."

"You ain't wearing that dress."

"Why not?"

"Do you want me to go back to prison?"

"What? No, of course not." I think all the orgasms have addled his brain.

"Then you can't wear that dress," he mutters, sliding his hands inside my skirt to grab my bottom.

"What's wrong with my dress?"

"There ain't enough of it." His eyes are narrowed, glittering with jealousy. "Anyone sees you in it and tries to touch you, I'm going to have a helluva time playing my guitar when it's up someone's ass."

I gape at him, caught between the desire to laugh because he looks like a grumpy bear and the desire to tell him he'll have a hard time sticking the guitar up someone's butt if it's already up his own. I shouldn't find it adorable that he's jealous over a dress. I shouldn't encourage him because he's a caveman...but I love that he doesn't want anyone else looking at me.

"You realize you're the one everyone is going to be looking at, right?" I ask him, just to make sure he's aware of that little fact. "I'll be hiding out in the corner while you're on stage, driving women crazy like you always do."

"They enjoy the music," he mutters.

"They also enjoy the man making the music. They literally throw their panties at you, Clayton."

He scowls at that reminder. "Wish they'd stop doing that," he rumbles. "Don't want any panties but yours, and I already got those in my pocket."

"You do not."

He releases my butt to dip his hand into his pocket. A second later, he pulls out the panties I wore yesterday.

"You can't carry my panties around in your pocket!" I hiss, my cheeks heating. I wondered where they went when I got up this morning and couldn't find them.

"Says who?" He quirks a brow at me, holding them up above my head when I try to grab them from him. "They smell like you. I'm keeping them."

"They're mine."

"Who made that pussy wet while you were in them, Addison?" he asks, securing one arm around my waist to keep me from climbing his body to steal them back. "I did. That means all that cream you left on them is mine."

"Clayton."

He nips at my throat. "You can have them back when I'm done with them."

"When you're done with them?"

"I got pictures of you and the panties you soaked for me, baby girl," he says. "You wear that dress tonight, and you'll be wearing these panties covered in my cum tomorrow."

Oh...geez. My womb clenches.

"I'm w-wearing my dress."

"Baby. Addison."

"I'm wearing my dress."

"You want me popping your cherry up against a wall in a closet with two hundred people listening in?" he growls in my ear. "Because that's exactly what's going to happen if you wear that tiny dress."

"Clayton." I mean it to be a chastisement, but it comes out as a needy moan.

"That dress is beautiful, but it ain't you, baby girl. When I look out at the crowd tonight, I want to see the sweet little angel that gets my dick so fucking hard," he says, his voice soft. "I've been looking for you in the crowd for seven months, hoping to see you smiling back at me."

"Clayton," I whisper, my irritation melting.

"You ain't got to prove anything to anyone, Addison, especially not to me," he says, placing little kisses all over my neck. "Just be you. You're perfect exactly the way you are. I don't want you changing for me or wearing a dress we both know you ain't going to be comfortable wearing."

"Okay," I whisper, unable to deny him when I know he's right. That dress isn't me.

"You deserve to be pampered and spoiled. Let me spoil you today."

"You don't have to do that. I don't...like you because of your money." The word love almost slips out before I can stop it. He hasn't said it yet. Am I allowed to say it first? Should I? What if he's not ready yet?

"You think I don't know that?" He hooks a finger under my chin, tipping my head back until my eyes meet his. "There ain't a materialistic bone in your body. But I've got millions sitting in a bank, and I've been dreaming of getting to spend them on you for months. Let me do that today."

How am I supposed to resist when he looks at me like I'm the only woman in the world? I can't believe I never questioned why he always wore his sunglasses. Riley and Cami were right, though. He wore them to keep anyone from noticing what's right there on his face, plain as day. He may not have said the words yet, but I feel them in my soul. He's in love with me.

"Okay," I whisper, giving him what he wants.

His little boy smile is all the reward I need.

Chapter Ten

"Jesus," I mutter, peeking out at the crowd in the ballroom. They're packed in like sardines, dripping jewels and sweating expensive champagne. Women outnumber the men in the crowd three to one. Kasen's on stage, crooning about his love life. The dance floor is packed.

The one woman I'm dying to see ain't out there yet, at least not that I've been able to find. She's been gone since eleven this morning. Didn't think about how long it'd take for her to get all dolled up for tonight. I'm missing her like a junkie misses the needle. She's in my blood now, running through it like whiskey. Only there ain't no diluting her or getting her out again.

I'm not a poetic man, but there's a certain beauty in knowing how irrevocably she's changed me. There are parts of my past I wish like hell I could change. I ain't ashamed of them anymore. She drained that right out of me. Touching her, holding her, loving her has brought me peace in ways I never expected. I can't love her like she deserves and cling to guilt and shame at the same time. It just ain't possible.

"Clayton Devine."

I turn to find a leggy blonde standing behind me, smiling like I'm her dinner. Like most of the women in the ballroom, she's dripping diamonds. Her gold dress hugs her body, her tits damn near spilling out the top of it. She's maybe thirty or thirty-five.

"It's so good to see you again," she purrs, rushing forward to fling her arms around me.

I stumble back a step, my hands lifted in the air so she doesn't get the wrong idea here and think I'm hugging her back. Whoever she is, she ain't Addison and I'm not touching her.

Until her lips land against my jaw, giving me no choice.

I grab her arms, firmly moving her away from me.

"Am I supposed to know you?" I growl, grimacing at the smell of her perfume. It's overpowering, and not in a good way. Addison's sweet smell is intoxicating. This shit makes me want to gag.

"You don't remember me?" Her face falls into a pout that's fake as a three-dollar bill.

I look her over again, but she still isn't familiar.

"Never seen you before."

Irritation flashes in her eyes. "We met at your show in Houston six months ago," she says, schooling her expression into what I reckon is supposed to be a flirty smile. "I won backstage passes. We talked for like, an hour. Melody Zamora."

Still don't recognize her. I meet a lot of fans. They mostly talk and I just nod along. Riley had the crew handing out backstage passes left and right on my last tour. Said it was a great way to interact with fans since I don't do social media. Maybe I need to be changing that if women like Melody are winning. I don't remember anyone getting handsy in Houston, but she's sure as hell trying right now.

"You really don't remember me?"

"I meet a lot of fans, ma'am," I murmur, trying not to be rude to her.

Her face falls into another fake pout.

"You can make it up to me," she says, trying to put her hand on my dick.

I take a step back, out of her reach.

"You can take me out to dinner after the show."

"You want to go out to dinner?" I growl in disbelief. She's lost her ever-loving mind.

Addison's soft intake of breath is the only warning I get that she's here. I whip my head around to look at her. My dick, which was just shriveling thanks to Melody, instantly turns to steel.

My God. I should have let her wear her tiny dress.

She looks like a goddess, draped in blue silk and shining bright as the sun. Like her dress last night, this one ties up around her neck. White lace runs around the top and then down under her arms to her waist, offering tantalizing glimpses of her creamy skin. The dress is form fitting all the way down her body before flaring out around the bottom part of her legs. Her hair is done up in curls that cascade from an elegant bun. Her eyes are dark and smoky, her lips a pretty pink.

She looks beautiful, exactly like the angel she is. She also looks mad enough to spit fire.

Her blue eyes practically scorch me alive when the crazy woman behind me slides a hand around my waist, pressing herself up against my body. Not to be disrespectful to women, but some of them are bitches. Melody is one of them.

Her damn perfume chokes me.

"Stop fucking touching me," I growl at her, jerking away.

She makes an offended sound, but I don't even care if I hurt her feelings.

"Addison, little one," I murmur, holding out a hand to her. "Come here."

She takes a step backward, shaking her head.

My heart threatens to crack in half. Surely she knows I didn't ask this woman to come back here with me? That I've never touched her in my life?

"You need to leave," she says to Melody, speaking calmly. "Now."

"I'm sorry," Melody says, being rude as hell. "Who are you?"

"No one."

"My future wife," I growl at the same time, stalking across the small room to Addison to pull her into my arms. She's stiff, rigid. She doesn't push me away though.

"You're marrying her?" Melody says in disbelief. "How old is she? Twelve?"

Addison doesn't even flinch. "I'm old enough to know throwing myself at a man who isn't interested is embarrassing," she says, her voice soft. "But who cares if he's with someone else when he's hot and rich, right?"

"I don't remember him saying no." Melody scowls at her.

"He didn't have to say it. It was obvious."

"Right. Like you'd know," Melody says, rolling her eyes.

"I do know because I know him," Addison says, not letting Melody make her catty. If she's anxious to be speaking up, she doesn't waver.

"So do I."

"No, you don't," Addison says, standing her ground and staking her claim on me boldly, without hesitation or fear.

She *knows* I'm hers and isn't afraid to let Melody know it either. "You listen to his music and see him on TV, and you think you know him. You don't. If you did, you would have seen that he clearly wasn't comfortable with you trying to touch him. You'd know that he'll never love you. He'll never touch you. Every part of him belongs to me. And in case it isn't obvious yet, I don't share."

"You little bitch," Melody hisses.

And I've heard enough. No one disrespects Addison, especially not in front of me.

"You heard my future wife," I growl at Melody. "Get the hell out of here and don't come back again. If I find you within one hundred feet of me or my girl, you won't like the consequences."

"Whatever. Keep your little girlfriend," she huffs. "You aren't my type anyway. I was just trying to do you a favor." She scowls at us and then storms off, pissed.

"Addison," I whisper as soon as she's gone, proud to bursting of my girl. I want to tumble her to the floor right here and worship her.

"I'm so mad," she says, her voice shaking.

"I didn't touch her," I promise.

"I know. You wouldn't do that to me."

"Then why are you mad, little one?"

"She touched you," she whispers, her voice a soft growl. "I didn't like it."

"Me either. My dick shriveled," I mutter, not lying to her. The only hands I want on me belong to the brave, beautiful woman currently in my arms. God could take everything from me, and I wouldn't complain. The money, the fame, my guitar. My voice. To keep Addison, there isn't a single thing I wouldn't sacrifice. Wouldn't even have to think about it either.

"Did you touch her before? In Houston?" she asks, her voice small.

"Hell no," I growl, shuddering at the thought. "You think I'd touch someone else when I'm so in love with you I can't see straight?"

"We weren't together six months ago," she whispers.

"I ain't been with anyone in years, and you've been mine since the day I met you. Wouldn't touch someone else when you're the only one my dick gets hard for," I growl, clearing that shit up now. I won't have her thinking I've been obsessing over her and sleeping around at the same time. If it wasn't going to be her, it wasn't going to be anyone. "You're the one my heart beats for. I love *you*, little one. I belong to *you*. You think I'm going to do anything to risk that? Never."

"Oh." She stands completely still for a long moment, long enough to make me worry she doesn't believe me, doesn't know how I feel about her. And then she tips her head back to look up at me. "You're in love with me."

It's not a question.

"Have been for seven months," I say anyway. Until two days ago, I thought I was hiding it well enough. Clearly not since everyone knew except the angel in my arms. I should have known better. The way I feel about her? There ain't no hiding the way my entire world comes alive when she's near.

"Me too," she says, her eyes bright. "I wanted to tell you this morning, but I wasn't sure if I was allowed to do that or if you would think it was too fast or..."

I cut her off by pressing my mouth to hers, kissing her long and deep. I don't stop until she's trembling in my arms and whimpering, trying to climb my body to get closer to me.

"I love you, little one."

"I–"

"I want to hear you say it for the first time when I'm inside you," I growl against her lips, cutting her off before she can say it. The first time I hear those words from her, I want it to be when I'm planting my kid in her belly, tying her to me irrevocably.

"Clayton."

"Tonight, baby girl. You tell me tonight."

"Okay," she agrees.

"This ole' country boy met an angel in Nashville, now she's the only thing that feels like home," I croon, my voice fading. I play the last few chords of *Two Lane Blacktop* and then look up from my guitar to see Addison staring at me from across the room, her eyes bright with moisture. Don't think she had any idea how easily she captivates me. No idea just how much I love every single thing about her. She does now.

All night, I've been singing to her, sharing every song I ever wrote about her.

That's exactly all of them since I met her.

"Y'all have a good night," I murmur to the crowd, tipping my head in a nod as they all clap and cheer. I set my guitar aside and hop off the stage, headed toward my girl. She's sitting near the back of the room with Kasen, Bentley, and their wives, looking like she ain't got a care in the world.

If she's anxious to be around so many people, it doesn't show. She walked around the stage, taking pictures while I was up there. Half the motherfuckers in this room couldn't keep their eyes off her tonight. Can't even blame them, as much as it pains my possessive ass to admit it.

She's glowing bright as the sun. Knowing I'm responsible for that, that I'm the reason she's so happy, is a hell of a thing. Took every bit of self-control I possess not to drop my guitar, scoop her up into my arms, and carry her out of here to see just how much brighter she'll glow when I'm inside her.

Love looks good on her. Hell, it looks like heaven on her. Not sure how I missed it for so long. She's always looked at me the same way, like I'm her hero. Even when she was too afraid to speak to me, she always looked at me like I hung the moon just for her. I guess we were both too afraid to hope. A man like me winning a girl like her? Didn't think I stood a chance in hell.

Knowing she felt the same way about me all along blows my mind. Had I sung to her before now, I would have realized. She couldn't keep her eyes off me all night. Even wiped a tear away a time or two. She's sweet as pie. And now she's all mine.

When I step up in front of the table, her eyes meet mine, her lips slightly parted.

"It's time to go," I murmur, holding out a hand to her. I don't even say hello to everyone else at the table. I can't. All I can think about is getting her upstairs and getting her on her back so I can finally hear her say she loves me.

"Bye, everyone," she says, not taking her eyes off me.

I pull her out of her seat, kissing her long and deep, just so everyone knows she's mine and I'm hers. A ripple of sound goes through the room. I hear several people asking who she is and what I'm doing with her. As if they have a say. As if they could ever hope to compete.

"I'm marrying her," I say, loud enough for everyone around us to hear. There won't be another Melody Zamora situation. My girl handled it like the queen she is, but it won't happen again. I won't have women upsetting her when they don't even exist to me.

"Obviously," Kasen mutters through laughter.

"Aww," Olivia says at the same time.

"He sounds like you," Cami says, laughing.

"That's because he's smart, little dove," Bentley says. "People say all kinds of things they don't have any business saying. Better to nip that shit in the bud up front."

"See ya," I mutter to them, pulling Addison away from the table.

"My camera!" she says.

"Shit." I spin around to grab it, only to find Cami already holding it out toward me, laughing. I take it from her and mumble a thanks. If she responds, I don't hear her. All my attention is focused on Addison. Her dress is backless. Those little dimples are visible again. I think she picked this one just to torture me, just because she could.

"I realized something tonight," Addison says once we're out of the ballroom. There aren't many people out in the hall, but she stays glued to my side, avoiding those who look in our direction.

A quick frown from me has them quickly looking elsewhere. My girl may have found her voice with me, but I know people still make her anxious. It makes me proud as hell to know she trusts me to keep her safe. It makes me just as proud to know she didn't question my loyalty to her for a single second with Melody.

"What did you realize, baby?" I ask, leading her through the hotel.

"I'm the angel in *Two Lane Blacktop*," she says. "I thought it was Riley and you were talking about how much you miss your bar, but you weren't. You changed the lyrics of the last line tonight because it's always been about me, hasn't it?"

I swipe my keycard to call the elevator and then turn to glare at the couple taking pictures of us from across the lobby. They quickly turn and hurry off in the opposite direction. The pictures will probably be all over the internet tomorrow. I'm surprised we made it this long without being photographed together.

"I need to hire security for you," I murmur to Addison, pulling her into the elevator and then into my arms. "Don't want anyone harassing you when you're trying to study."

She scrunches up her face and then nods. "Okay."

I quirk a brow, surprised she's agreeing so easily. She gave me hell about her dress today. "You ain't going to kick up a fuss?"

"Having someone with me will keep you from stressing out." She bites her lip, suddenly leery. "Um, can it be a woman?"

"I'll see what I can do," I promise. If a woman makes her feel more comfortable, I'll find one who can keep her safe without making her feel more anxious than the photographers and looky-loos they're there to keep away.

"Then no, I'm not going to kick up a fuss." She smiles when she says *kick up a fuss*.

Addison may have been born and raised in the south like me, but she talks proper. Me? Not so much. I may not look quite country enough for some people, but I damn sure sound it. Don't bother me none, and it doesn't seem to bother Addison either. I didn't grow up in a fancy town like Nashville. I was born and raised in a sleepy little backwoods town twenty minutes outside of Little Rock. We had more cows than people and enough crops to provide for half the state. I spent my days playing pool at my father's bar with farmers and pipeliners.

"I missed you today," Addison murmurs, laying her head on my chest once the elevator jolts into motion.

"Did you and Olivia have fun?" I ask, kneading the back of her neck with my thumbs. Olivia went with her today so she wouldn't be alone. I think Kasen wanted to spoil his wife a little bit too. She's pregnant and has been dealing with a sick baby. He was on board as soon as I called him this morning to ask.

"Mmhmm."

The elevator glides to a stop.

"They're all about you."

"What?"

I lead her off the elevator into the suite before I respond. "The songs. My whole last album was about you. Imagine my next one will be too."

"Seriously? Even *Peaceful Easy*?"

"Don't believe in much beyond her shy smile and that peaceful easy feeling," I murmur the line, reaching up to run my thumb across her bottom lip.

"*Black Falls*?"

"Cornflower blue shining like diamonds behind black falls." I remove the clip from her hair, watching as it tumbles down around her face like a midnight waterfall. "Pretty baby don't know how tempting she is. She gave a man a glimpse of heaven and sent him straight to hell."

She scrunches up her face at me. "I don't like that one. It's sad. I don't like that you think you aren't worthy of me or that me being with you will mess up my life. You're a good man, Clayton. One of the best I know."

"Starting to see things your way," I promise. "But I still got a lot of atoning to do for the sins I committed."

"Tell me about them?" she asks, slipping her hand into mine once I set her camera on the table.

"My old man raised me," I say, guiding her toward the bedroom. This ain't a conversation I particularly want to have with her, but I won't hide the truth from her. "He had a brother, Danny. Growing up, Danny was my hero. And then he and my dad had a falling out and I wasn't allowed to see him anymore. I resented the hell out of my old man for it. So when I turned sixteen, I started sneaking around behind his back to see my uncle."

"Why didn't they get along?"

"Danny ran an outlaw motorcycle club," I murmur, flipping on the lights for the bedroom. "My old man knew which way the wind was blowing and didn't want me getting involved in it. But I was young and dumb and didn't know any better. Danny convinced me that my old man was just being unreasonable. I joined up when I was seventeen. My old man found out, told me if I was going to throw my life away, he wasn't going to watch it happen. If I left, I wasn't welcome back. I left anyway."

"That's terrible," Addison says, letting me pick her up to sit her on the bed.

"He wasn't wrong," I murmur, dropping to my knees in front of her to remove her shoes. "He knew his brother a helluva lot better than I did. Danny talked a good game, made me think he actually cared about me. It was all just talk, said to convince me that what he wanted me to do wasn't that bad. Drugs, guns, booze, I stole and sold them all. It put money in my pocket, so I didn't question what we were doing."

"He should have looked out for you."

"Danny was married. His wife was young, a real sweet girl. She was a good friend, but I didn't know he was beating on her."

"Oh no," Addison whispers, her face falling.

"He beat her bad one night when she was pregnant. She came to me for help, covered in bruises and blood. Had their daughter with her," I say, stroking my finger across her instep. Her polish is blue now, matches her dress. "I'd just got home from a pickup, had a little over twenty thousand dollars of the club's money. I gave it to her, got her out of there."

"Good," Addison says.

"And then I confronted Danny about it. He said he felt awful about it. Swore he didn't know she was pregnant and that it was just the alcohol talking, that he'd just lost his head," I mutter. "Acted like I did the right thing and that he wasn't mad about it. I shoulda known better than to believe he would let it ride. No one crossed him without paying dearly. My next job, the police were waiting as soon as I crossed the state line."

"He set you up?"

"Mmhmm. For murder."

Addison gasps.

"He'd followed me, waited until I got the drugs and left, and then he shot our supplier with my gun. My fingerprints were all over it. He would have succeeded in pinning the murder on me had a witness not come forward to clear me. The supplier's neighbor saw the supplier walk me to the door, saw me hop on my bike and take off. Saw my uncle arrive. Had it not been for him, I'd still be in prison, serving life for a murder I didn't commit. Instead, I did five years for the drug charges."

"That's really awful, Clayton," Addison whispers, her expression full of sympathy.

"My old man came to my sentencing. First time I'd seen him in seven years. Last time too. He died while I was serving my time. Cancer."

"Clayton." She slides off the bed onto my lap, wrapping her arms around me. "I'm so sorry."

"Me too," I murmur, rubbing her back. "When I got out, I started working, taking any job I could find. Saved every penny I could to buy his bar back. Figured I owed him that. I finally saved enough, and that's where Riley found me a year later. I let her convince me to come out here and give Nashville a shot."

"What happened to your uncle?"

"He was on the run for a while. Finally died in a shoot-out about a year into my sentence," I murmur. "Most of the club ended up doing their own sentences."

"I'm so sorry you went through all that."

"A man died because I crossed my uncle. My old man lost his bar and died alone because I chose Danny over him. I wasn't a good man, little one. I was selfish, and arrogant, and did a lot of shit I ain't proud of doing. But I ain't letting that eat at me anymore. I figure if God sent me one of his angels, he must see something in me worth saving."

"You've always been worth it." She lifts up, kissing all along my throat. "Always, Clayton."

Even after knowing the whole sordid story of my life, she still isn't running from me. She still sees something in me worth loving. I don't know what I did to deserve her, but I ain't going to be dumb enough to prove her wrong. If my angel thinks I'm worth loving, I'm going to make damn sure I am the man she sees. But before she makes that choice and ties herself to me, she ought to know just how deep my obsession runs.

"I got something to show you. And I don't know how you're going to take it."

"Show me," she says without hesitation.

"Hop up on the bed," I murmur, wrapping my hands around her waist to lift her to her feet.

She perches on the edge of the bed, sitting all proper, like an actual queen.

I rise to my feet, stripping off my tie and button down, the only concessions to civility I was willing to make tonight. She licks her lips, staring at me. She's cute as a button, looking at me like I'm a snack. I'm not a vain man, but I know what women say about me. I don't work out to look good. I do it to stay in shape. There wasn't a whole helluva lot to do in prison except work out. I liked the comfort of having a routine and the clarity I found when

I was doing something other than staring at the four walls of my cell.

For the last seven months, working out has been more out of self-preservation than anything. I needed to work off the sexual frustration so I didn't move too fast with Addison and fuck it up. That ends tonight.

I turn slowly, putting my back to her so she can see just how mine she is, just how hers I am.

"Clayton," she gasps. "Is that-?"

"You?" I ask. For me, it's been her since day one. I reckon it always will be. Do you hear me complaining? Hell no. I'm thanking my lucky stars. "Yeah, little one, it's you."

Chapter Eleven

Addison

I stare at Clayton's back, trying to process the fact that my face stares back at me in vivid color. I'm inked into his skin, a permanent part of him. The tattoo is beautiful and lifelike. Whoever did it is incredibly talented.

My lips are pursed in it, a breath away from kissing him. Only he's a ghost, one side of his face floating away from the image like dandelions. It's as sad as it is beautiful.

I slide off the bed, reaching out to trace his face. "You look so young here," I whisper. "Tell me why you're a ghost."

"He represents the man I could have been had I made different choices when they counted," he murmurs. "He's the man I wish I could be for you now. One who is worthy of you."

"You're worthy of me now, Clayton."

"I'm not," he says, turning to face me. His expression is somber, so serious. "But I'll spend every damn minute of the day trying to be worthy of you. You'll never have a reason to doubt me or how crazy I am about you. I know jack shit about relationships, Addison, but I'll learn."

"You're doing pretty great already," I whisper. "Last night is the first time I slept in the dark since the night I got lost in the woods. It's the first time I felt safe in the dark. Today is the first time I haven't felt like running to hide when someone looked at me. That's because of you, Clayton. Because you make me feel like I'm strong enough, brave enough, and good enough just like I am."

How can I be afraid of what anyone else will think when the only man who matters to me has heard me stutter, seen me freeze, and still looks at me as if I'm the center of the universe? I may never feel completely comfortable speaking to people. I may still freeze up sometimes or say nothing at all...but I know that even if that happens, he'll never be disappointed. He'll never laugh or judge me or ask why I can't be *more*. He loves me.

"You're all of those things, little one," he murmurs, tugging me closer to his body. "You always have been. I love you."

"Then love me," I whisper, leaning up to press my mouth to his. His lips part, his beard tickles my chin. And then his tongue touches mine and I get lost in him. He pulls me closer, until we're pressed so tightly together not even air moves between us. We're two bodies, sharing one soul, joined at the lips.

I run my hands over his chest, moaning as I feel his naked flesh for the first time. His body is rock hard, his chest covered in dark hair. He isn't ripped like a body builder, with muscles crammed on top of muscles. But every inch of him feels as if he were cut from marble. It's funny. He's stripped me bare and touched every inch of me, left me drowning in so much pleasure I never questioned why I was the only one naked.

This time, I get to explore.

We undress one another between long kisses that grow hotter, hungrier. By the time I'm naked, I'm trembling. Those trembles turn to full body quakes when he yanks his boxers down and kicks them off. His erection juts proudly from a tight thatch of dark hair, long and hard. He's beautiful. The broad head is red, glistening with precum. A large purple vein runs down the underside of his cock.

"Shit," he groans when I reach for him. He plants his feet, locking his legs as if to keep him upright as I explore.

I run my fingers down his shaft, feel the weight of his balls in my hand. He's so darn big and beautiful everywhere. I want to taste him like he did me, make him crazy like he did me.

"Lay down," I say, releasing him to place my hands on his chest.

"You're a bossy little thing," he says, but he gives me what I want. He sits on the edge of the bed and then swings his legs around, laying flat. Well, most of him lays flat. His cock juts into the air, standing proud.

I crawl onto the bed with him, kneeling at his side.

"What are you up to, little one?" he asks me.

"Exploring."

My favorite little boy smile greets me.

I lean down to kiss him. He lets me control it. I take advantage of his obedience, slipping my tongue inside his mouth to stroke against his own. I run my hands down his chest at the same time, feeling him beneath my palms.

He groans when I rake my nails over his nipples. He makes the same sound when I run my hand down his abdomen and grip his erection. I'm not sure what I'm doing, but I squeeze him, working my hand up and down his shaft. Judging by the way he growls my name and arches his hips, I'm not doing it wrong.

I kiss a trail down his chest and stomach, my lips lingering on each of his tattoos. He has so many of them. His body trembles beneath me. I marvel at this...at how easily I can unravel him. He's larger than life to me, a legitimate superstar. But the girl who rarely speaks to strangers and has always been afraid of the dark can make him tremble and shake. It's a heady feeling.

"Baby," he groans, arching his hips, impatient and greedy for me to kiss him there.

I don't. At least not right away. I kiss all over his lower abdomen, follow the V of his hips. I nip at his skin, making him growl. The same growl rumbles from him when my cheek brushes up against his erection. I turn my face and press a kiss to his shaft.

"Jesus Christ," he grits out, his stomach clenching.

I laugh and kiss him there again, running my lips up the side of his shaft. I flick my tongue out to touch the slit at the top, moaning as his flavor bursts on my tongue. It's salty and sweet at the same time. I back off and blow against the head.

"Suck me," Clayton groans. "Let me have that sweet mouth."

"No. I'm not done yet."

He growls at me.

I kiss all over his thighs. They're just as big as the rest of him, just as hard.

"You know I'm going to fuck you into next week when you're done teasing me, right?" he growls.

I lift my eyes to his.

"Going to fuck you until you're screaming, little one," he warns me. The wicked promise reflects in his eyes, scorching me. "Stop teasing and suck me."

I shake my head, kissing all along his shaft again. He shifts restlessly beneath me, fighting the urge to take control and make me obey. His groans and curses sound like music to me. They grow louder when I take him into my mouth.

He's so hard yet so soft at the same time. I love the way he feels in my mouth and the way he tastes. I love the way he tips his head back and shouts my name. Trying to take all of him is impossible. I don't even manage to fit half of him in my mouth before I have to pull back to take a breath.

"That mouth," he growls.

"You taste good." I take him into my mouth again. I've never done this before, but I've read enough dirty books to have a general idea. I play with him in my mouth, moving up and down his shaft, using my tongue. I move to his balls, running my lips over them.

"Fuck, little one. Please," he moans. "Please."

I glance up to see his eyes blazing with heat, his expression one of intense pleasure/pain. He's wrecked for me, his self-control completely gone. And God, he's beautiful.

I take him into my mouth again, plunging down on him as far as I can go.

His hands sink into my hair, gathering it up in a fist. It's my turn to moan when he pumps his hips, causing him to slide in and out of my mouth. He grips my hair tight enough to make it sting, but somehow, that only makes me want to please him more, makes me ache more.

He holds me still, pumping his hips and cursing. The filthiest things tumble from his lips, gritted between curses and pants as he takes my mouth. No one has ever spoken to me the way he does, said the things he says. I love his filthy mouth way more than I probably should.

I can't help it though. He doesn't make me guess what he's thinking about or how he feels. He just tells me, words spilling from him in a growl of sound that grates against my womb. I chafe my thighs together, trying to ease the ache he's causing, but it's no use.

"That hot little mouth," he growls. "I want to feel you choking on my cock."

I claw at his thighs, more than willing to give him whatever he wants.

He thrusts into my mouth again, deep enough to touch the back of my throat. He holds me there for a moment, long enough to make my eyes water and my heart race. I'm not afraid though. Maybe I should be. Maybe that's what a virgin is supposed to feel. But I don't. I know he won't hurt me. Everything he does to me makes me feel so freaking good.

If that's wrong, then so be it.

He expels himself from my mouth all at once, his hips landing back against the bed. I cry out in disappointment, not ready to be done with him yet.

"Stop fighting me," he growls when I try to get my hands on him again. He picks me up, rolling until I'm pinned beneath him, my hands held captive in one of his. His mouth closes around my right breast.

"Clayton!" I shout, shocked when he bites me. It doesn't hurt. Pleasure rips through me. I try to arch beneath him, to get closer, but he's holding me down, refusing to let me go.

"It's my turn now," he says before biting my other nipple. "I get to play with this sexy little body, touch you however I want."

I whimper, already knowing he's going to wreck me.

I'm not wrong. He works his way down my body like a force of nature, possessing every inch of me. Owning every inch of me. He bites and kisses and sucks until I'm squirming and pleading for relief. He doesn't touch me where I need him though. He pays me back for teasing him fivefold. He pries my legs apart, fitting his big body between them.

His breath touches my center.

I fight against his hold again, trying to get my hands on him, to get him to touch me where I need him. He doesn't let me go though. It's almost offensive how easily he holds me down. How he doesn't even break a sweat even though I'm already panting for breath.

He's big and rough and rude and I don't ever want him to stop tormenting me this way. I never want to leave this bed or stop feeling like I'm going to explode into tiny, molten pieces of desire.

"Clayton!" I scream when he buries his face in my center. His beard abrades the sensitive skin of my inner thighs. His lips wrap around my clit, sucking it into his mouth. He eats me like a starving animal, growling and cursing.

I explode apart within seconds, too turned on to even try to slow it down or stop it. I don't think I could even if I tried. He's in charge of my body, of my pleasure, and he knows it better than I do. He eats me loudly as stars rupture behind my eyelids and the whole world flips and spins out of focus.

"Again," he growls as soon as I fall limp beneath him.

Within seconds, I'm racing up the hill again, his talented tongue touching parts of me I didn't even know existed. He presses it to my back entrance, and I shatter again, wailing this time.

He still doesn't stop. I writhe beneath him, squirming to get away from his mouth and to get closer all at the same time.

"You don't come again until I decide to let you," he says, backing off when I'm right on the edge again. He nuzzles my clit, placing sweet little kisses to my mound. As soon as the flutters ease off, he goes right back to owning my body, licking and sucking at me until I'm trembling again, my inner muscles fluttering, clenching.

I'm so close. So, so close.

"Please," I sob.

"No." He lifts me up higher and then eases off only to lift me higher again. Until I'm sobbing his name, tears leaking from the corners of my eyes because I can't take any more.

If I don't come soon, I think I might actually die. Time stands still, ceases to exist. All that's left is him and the pleasure/pain wracking my body.

I tremble on the ledge, sobbing because I know he isn't going to let me go over. I teased him, took control. He's reminding me who is really in charge. He's bossy and dominant, commanding my body because he can. Because he knows it's his to do with as he wants. Because he's obsessed with every inch of me.

"Now," he growls this time, flicking his tongue against my clit in rapid strikes.

Not a single sound leaves my lips when I shatter. Making sound is impossible when every atom of my body ruptures apart at the seams in an explosion big enough to leave me reeling. I drown in pleasure, coming so hard it makes my head hurt.

Clayton rises up over me, yanking me partially into his lap. I feel his erection against my center.

"Hang on to me," he mutters. "This is going to hurt."

I can't make my hands work to obey his command. I can't make any of my body do what I want it to do. All I can do is float.

He lines up at my entrance and thrusts into me. I feel the sharp pain as my hymen tears, but it feels muted and far away. Clayton feels it too. He cries out, the sound distressed and triumphant at the same time.

"Fuck, little one," he growls, leaning down to bury his face in my throat. "I'm sorry. Christ, I'm sorry. I can't stop." He writhes on top of me in shallow thrusts, panting in my ear, begging for forgiveness in one breathe and telling me how good I feel in the next.

"I'm f-fine," I finally manage to say. The pain is already gone, dulled because all I feel is awe and him. He's inside me. I'm his. How could that ever feel anything less than perfect?

He groans my name, seeking out my lips with his. His lips taste like me, but I don't mind. I kiss him back willingly, eagerly as he makes love to me. He keeps his body pressed tight to mine, rolling his hips as he thrusts in and out of me in a slow glide. I feel him everywhere, surrounding me.

"You're so damn perfect, little one. Say it now. Please," he pleads.

"I love you, Clayton."

He cries out wordlessly, throwing his head back as if the words overwhelm him.

"I love you," I say again. And then again, "I love you."

He roars my name, unraveling for me again. His thrusts pick up speed until he's pounding into me, fucking me so hard the bed shakes and I can't catch my breath. I sob his name, tell him I love him in broken cries that only make him go harder, deeper.

I've never felt anything like him before. He's so big I feel like he's going to split me open. But it doesn't hurt. I feel full, but that doesn't hurt either. He keeps hitting some spot inside that makes my eyes roll back in my head. I claw down his back, bite his shoulder.

The cord snaps and I fall backward into pleasure. It rolls through me in warm waves, spreading bliss all throughout my system.

"I love you, I love you," I cry through it, clinging to Clayton.

He roars my name and then I feel his hand around my throat. He pins me to the bed beneath him without cutting off my air supply. He takes me in ruthless strikes that rattle and shake the bed beneath me. I rock against him, helpless to do anything other than take it. And I do. Every hard thrust. They crack me apart, leave me writhing in ecstasy.

He comes with another roar, shouting my name into the room so loudly it echoes in the corners. His seed spills into me in heavy spurts, spreading deep inside. He pumps his hips through it, moaning my name, chanting it into my throat.

"Addison, Addison. God, baby. God. What are you doing to me?" he asks, but I don't think he expects an answer. I don't have one for him because I feel it too. He's still inside me, still hard. And I want him again, want him endlessly.

I run my hands all over his back as he pants and trembles in my arms, completely undone. Ruined for me, just like he said he would be. I am too. Completely wrecked. Nothing has ever felt better. Nothing has ever felt this right.

"I love you."

"Little one," he breathes, pressing his sweaty head to my chest. His lips touch my racing heart. "Mine. You're mine now."

"I've been yours all along," I whisper back.

"I can't believe you tattooed me on you," I whisper, tracing my fingers down his back. He's on his stomach beside me, his head turned and his eyes on me. We're still in the bed, still a mess of sweat and our juices. I never want to move. Never want to leave.

"Don't you know, little one?" he asks, his lips curving into my favorite grin. "You're the only thing in Nashville that feels like home to me. I needed you with me, even if all I could have was your face inked on my skin."

"Clayton," I whisper, my heart melting.

He reaches out to stroke my cheek. "Do you want a big wedding?"

"No. I just want you."

"You have that already."

"Maybe some flowers."

He smiles. "I think I can arrange that. I want to release a statement."

"Why?"

"So the whole world knows you're mine."

"Crazy man," I say, smiling back at him. "I'm guessing they already know. It's been a few hours since you said you were marrying me downstairs. It's probably all over the internet by now."

"Good," he says with a grunt, flipping onto his side and then hooking an arm around my waist to pull me up against him. My bottom nestles against his groin. His erection stirs. "Then they won't be surprised when you move in with me tomorrow."

"What?" I freeze.

"You're moving in with me tomorrow," he says. "I need you in my bed. Otherwise I'll worry you ain't sleeping well, that you're afraid. Gotta keep you close so I can watch out for you. It's my job now."

"Does that mean I get to watch out for you?"

"You want to watch out for me?"

"Mmhmm. Gotta keep crazy women away from you," I say, scowling at the thought of another situation like tonight. If I didn't trust him so completely, that could have been bad. And I know it's bound to happen again. He's a freaking superstar. Women will never stop trying to throw themselves at him.

He chuckles, his breath tickling my neck. "You were sexy as hell today, staking your claim on me. You're a fierce little queen when you want to be."

"You make me feel like a queen."

"Good," he grunts. "Then I'm doing my job right because you are a queen. A single crook of your finger, and you could command me to do anything."

"Oh yeah?" I wriggle until I'm able to roll over in his arms to face him.

"Definitely," he whispers, resting his forehead against mine. His nose slides along the side of mine. "I'm yours, little one. Command me. Wreck me."

"I'd rather just love you," I whisper back.

"Yeah?" His lips seek mine. "Then love me, my queen."

"I will," I promise. "Forever."

Epilogue

Clayton

Five Years Later

"Addison! Addison! Are you excited? When did you find out?"

Cameras flash, momentarily blinding me. I growl and throw out an arm, trying to stop the crowd of paparazzi from swarming my wife.

"Move back," I growl, tucking her close to my body to keep hold of her. It's a jungle out here and I don't want to lose her in the crowd. "Give her some room!"

"It's okay," she whispers and then I feel her hand in mine. She squeezes it tightly, trying to reassure me that she's fine. That ain't what I'm worried about though. I'm worried about the babies in her belly. She's three months pregnant with twins, and these assholes are far too close.

They've been relentless since they found out she's pregnant again. It's enough to make me crazy. And not in a good way. My wife can't seem to go anywhere without someone taking her picture, documenting every move she makes. Riley keeps assuring me they'll stop kicking up a fuss about us sooner or later. But for the moment, they seem to be as obsessed with my wife and babies as I am.

You'd think this was the first time I put a baby in her belly instead of the third.

Addison handles the constant onslaught well. Far better than I do if I'm being honest. She says she doesn't worry about them because she knows she doesn't have to speak if she doesn't want to do so. They don't really expect her to talk to them anyway. After five years, they've become accustomed to the fact that she don't like talking to them.

She's grown a lot over the years, becoming more confident and less anxious. She says that's because she knows she's safe with me. I think it's because she's finally realized that she ain't that helpless little girl who stumbled out of the woods into a viper's nest of nosy reporters. She's all woman, powerful in her own right. She speaks when she wants to speak and don't apologize when she doesn't. She knows she don't owe anyone a damn thing. Her security team helps make sure the rest of the world know she doesn't owe them shit either.

Most people respect her privacy enough to leave her alone. She didn't sign up to be hounded when she married me. Ten years ago, that might not have meant as much as it does today. But the world has changed since popstars were terrorized just for being popstars. People are more respectful now, even paparazzi.

Still, I can't wait until they find someone else to annoy and leave me and my wife in peace again.

"Back up!" her main security guard, Maya, shouts, surging through the crowd to clear a path for us. The rest of her team pours out of the building behind her, blocking a path so I can hurry Addison through the doors.

Photographers press up against the glass, trying to take photos through it.

"Why are they all here?" I growl to no one in particular. It's been a while since a crowd this big swarmed us.

"Maybe because you knocked her up with twins," Riley says, coming around the corner. "And then decided to announce it by shouting it at the last photographer who followed you."

"They were crowding her."

"There were two of them, Clayton," Riley says, rolling her eyes, which makes Addison giggle.

I turn a glare on my wife, who bites her lip to hide her laughter. She tells me all the time that I go crazy when she's pregnant, and maybe that's true. I worry incessantly about her and the babies. They're my life in every way that matters.

They've brought so much light into my life, it's hard to remember how dark it was before I claimed Addison as mine. Every damn day, I thank God for putting her in my path, for trusting me with her. I know how important she is, and I guard her and our boys close.

Sue me if reporters don't like it.

Sometimes, I hate that I ever said yes to Riley. I hate that people follow my wife around, and that they take pictures of my kids. Other times, I thank my lucky stars for Riley and this new life of mine. Without it, I never would have found Addison. I never would have found peace.

I'd still be strumming my guitar in the back of an old rundown bar, trying to measure up to the man who raised me and forget the one who almost destroyed me. I wouldn't be here now, with my pregnant wife looking edible in her yoga pants and t-shirt, her baby bump showing and my ring on her finger. I wouldn't have been able to afford that four-carat diamond that looks so good on her.

The last five years of my life have been the best years of my life. Being able to touch Addison whenever I want is heaven on earth. Getting to pick her up at the end of the day, or meet her here for lunch, cuddling with her on the couch, or holding her when she sleeps...there are a thousand little moments that still fill me with awe.

My favorite memories are those I've made with her and our sons. The boys look just like her. They're four and two, and they bring so much joy to our lives. They're both wild, always running around, always up to something. I love it though.

The moment they go down, I'm on their mama like white on rice. The way her eyes darken when she's turned on, the sound she makes when I spank her. How she sobs when I'm eating her, and the way she feels wrapped around me. Ain't no man alive who has it better. I spend most of my time inside my wife, teaching her all that dirty shit she's still too innocent to know. She ain't innocent when we're in bed. She's a kinky little thing, more than willing to let me do whatever I want to do to her. She enjoys every minute of it.

I let her play when she wants, let her take control and torment me. I'll never admit it, but I live for those moments when she's wrecking me with her mouth and hands. She's a goddess, and I'm her willing acolyte, fanatic in my worship. Every day, my obsession with her grows. I think about her constantly, want to be with her incessantly. There ain't a force in heaven or hell strong enough to drag me away from her.

Our boys love her just the same. As far as they're concerned, their mama hung the moon. She can't do any wrong, and she knows everything. She's an incredible mom. There isn't a single thing about our boys that she don't know. I am in awe of her and how much love she brings us. She seems to have an endless supply of it.

"Why are we here?" I ask Riley, ignoring the way she's smirking at me like she thinks I'm funny. She don't like the paparazzi following us anymore than I do. She's protective of my wife. She hired her on after her internship ended. Said she'll always have a place here. And she's had a place here for the last five years.

When she's here, I never have to worry if she's all right. I know she is. Riley and Cash consider her family, so do Cami and Bentley. I'm here most of the time anyway. Where else would I be when my wife and our sons are here?

Only it's better than it was before we went to Chattanooga five years ago. Because she talks to me now. I get to touch her now. I no longer sit coffee on her desk and walk away. I give her coffee. She gives me kisses. Duke, our two-year-old, frequently spends his time at her desk with her. He's not a big fan of daycare. Like his mama, he's quiet around strangers, timid. He's happiest when he's close to her.

"I don't know," Riley says. "Why are you here?"

I frown at her. She's the one who called me.

"Why are we here?" she asks my wife.

I turn to look at Addison, who smiles at me.

"Come on and I'll show you," she says, grabbing me by the hand and pulling me toward the elevator leading up to Riley's offices on the fourth floor.

Riley falls into step with us. The security team hangs back, staying down here to keep cameras out of the building. Hopefully they'll be gone by the time we leave so they don't follow us. They did that so often in the beginning, I stopped taking my bike anywhere. Having Addison on the back of it with paparazzi following us made me anxious as hell.

Addison loves being on the back of my bike though. When we can get away, I love taking her up in the mountains and making love to her on the back of it. She looks so damn good sprawled across it with that ass in the air.

By the time we reach Riley's floor, Addison is practically dancing in place, excited about whatever she wants to show us. She drags me toward Cami's desk. Cami grins at her and hands her an envelope, not saying anything.

"Thanks!" Addison takes the envelope and then drags me toward Riley's office.

"I need better shoes," Riley mutters from behind me.

We're barely in her office before Addison shoves the envelope at me.

"Surprise!" she says, grinning big enough to split her cheeks.

I look at the envelope and frown at the return address. "What is this?"

"Open it."

I glance at my wife and then back down at the envelope before tearing it open. A thick stack of papers is inside, folded neatly. An official seal is stamped on the corner of it. I slowly open the packet, folding it so it's flat. *Order of Expungement* is typed in bold face across the top.

"What did you do, baby girl?" I whisper, shocked as I scan through the document. It's a bunch of legal jargon, but I know enough to understand the significance. My criminal record has been sealed.

"You aren't that man anymore," Addison whispers, pushing her way into my arms. "I've known it for a long time. Riley knows it. Even you know it." She taps the sheaf of papers in my hand. "Now the state of Arkansas knows it too. Your record is sealed, Clayton. No one will ever find it now."

"Jesus," I whisper, not sure what to say as awe courses through me in a powerful flood. It's been a long time since I felt shame about who I was and the things I did. But there's always been a little hint of worry that someone would go digging into my past and find the skeletons hanging there. That they'd drag them out into the light, let the whole world see the things I did. That they'd all know I could never hope to be worthy of my wife, our boys, or the life I live.

Riley and Cash did what they could to bury it when Riley signed me. But they couldn't make it go away completely. Now, it's gone. Done. Over with.

"Jesus," I whisper again, holding the papers out to Riley. As soon as she takes them, I've got my mouth on my wife, kissing her hard and deep. Emotion courses through me, powerful and raw. My heart expands, making more room for her and the way I feel about her.

"You're free, Clayton," she whispers against my lips. I taste tears there, but I don't know if they're hers or if they're mine. Don't suppose it matters one way or another.

"No, little one," I say, resting my forehead against hers. "I was free the day you looked into my eyes and told me I was worthy of you. That's the day I started living again, the day I started hoping again. I've been free every day since. This just makes it official."

"Clayton," she sobs.

I wrap myself around her, holding her tight as she cries.

"I love you," she whispers.

"My heart beats for you," I say in return. It's nothing but the truth. My heart beat for the first time the day I met her. It's beat like a drum for her every day since. I don't even have to wonder if it'll always be that way. I already know it will.

Love isn't strong enough for the way I feel about her. Obsession isn't deep enough. This woman is my soul, the part of me that nothing and no one else could ever come close to touching. I'm hers to command. Completely. Irrevocably. Forever.

Author's Note

I f you enjoyed Black Velvet, please consider leaving a review! They are so helpful for authors.

If you haven't read Laney and Weston's story, Cutie Pie, it is now available. You can also read Riley and Cami's stories in the His Bride series!

Cutie Pie

Excerpt

"Excuse me? Mr. Davies?" a sweet voice calls as soon as I poke my head out into the arena.

It's already packed full of fans, a sea of yellow and black staring back at me.

Jesus. Why are so many of them female tonight?

If they're all here over this date shit, I'm killing Coach and Kelsey.

I glance over my shoulder, intending to tell whoever is calling my name that I've got shit to do, only to come to a dead stop when I spot her standing just on the other side of the boards. Even my heart stops beating. For one long moment, everything stops. I gape like a fucking crazy person, my mouth hanging open like this is some cartoon. But fuck me. I can't help it.

If angels are real, this sweet little thing is one of them. Her curly hair is so blonde it's almost white. It frames her round face, setting off the bluest eyes I've ever seen and her pink cheeks. Her full bottom lip is caught between her teeth, red where she's been biting on it.

Not even the bulky Predators hoodie she's wearing hides her incredible tits, or her generous curves. The number over her chest—number 84...*my* number—has my dick turning to steel. Which is a problem since I'm wearing a cup.

"Can I speak to you for a moment?" she asks me in the softest voice I've ever heard.

"Heads up!" Theo Kline shouts at the same time.

I turn just enough to see the puck whipping through the air in our direction. She doesn't see it. Her eyes are locked on the ice at my feet.

I make a split-second decision and lunge forward, throwing myself between her and the puck coming at her like a missile.

People think helmets mean we don't feel hits to the head. They're wrong. A hard enough hit hurts like a mother-fucker regardless of the helmet and can still cause serious problems. This is one of those that hurt.

The puck cracks me in the back of the head hard enough to rattle my teeth. The hit knocks me off-balance. I stumble into the boards, which puts me within inches of the heavenly little blonde who smells like strawberries. I grunt, my eyes stinging from the pain.

"Oh my gosh!" she cries out, her sweet voice full of distress. "Are you okay?"

"Yeah, fine," I lie, waving off her concern. I'm not fine. Jesus Christ. That shit hurt like a motherfucker.

"You good, Wes?" Theo shouts, skating up behind me.

"Fine!" I scoop the puck up and launch it toward him before turning back to the girl...angel...goddess. Good lord. How did something so beautiful escape to this world?

"Are you okay?" I ask...growl, really. It's hard to think and look at her at the same time.

"Me?" She blinks the longest lashes I've ever seen. "You're the one who just took a puck to the back of the head."

"Believe me, I know," I growl, my head and my cock aching in time to one another. Who needs chastity belts when you can buy a cup? Whoever said you can't get an erection in these fuckers was a liar. My dick feels like he's trying to Hulk smash through the damn thing to get to this angel.

"What's your name?" I ask, trying like hell not to think about my dick.

"Laney. Um, Laney Briggs."

"Laney," I murmur, just to feel that name on my tongue. Until I get other parts of her there, the name will have to do. "What can I do for you other than taking a puck to the head?"

"I, well...um...I don't know how to even say it."

"You want me to sign something for you?" I grin at her, more than willing to put my name wherever she wants it.

I never sign body parts, but I'll make an exception for that gorgeous body. Especially those tits. "I'll definitely sign those tits."

Her eyes widen, her mouth popping open in shock.

"Shit," I mutter. I said that out loud. Jesus Christ. If I have a concussion, I'm killing Theo and whoever shot the puck to him. "That didn't come out right. You're fucking me all up."

"Excuse me?"

"I can't fucking think around you," I growl, trying to explain. "My head and my dick hurt."

Call me crazy, but I don't think I'm making this sound any better.

"Wow," Laney mutters, her face turning red. Her eyes flash fire at me. "Has anyone ever told you that you're kind of an asshole?"

Yes, frequently.

"I didn't mean..."

"I don't want your autograph," she huffs, crossing her arms, which only serves to lift those tits higher. "Especially not on my boobs. No wonder they're raffling off a date with you. You may be pretty to look at, but once you open your mouth, you kind of ruin the whole thing. I can't believe I let Addison talk me into entering that stupid contest."

Am I supposed to find her hot right now? I'm not, am I?

"Wait. You entered the Win a Date thing?"

She sniffs instead of answering, but the way she shifts her gaze away from me is all the confirmation I need. She did enter. If I take her on the date, I can avoid puck bunnies and convince her to marry me and give me babies and shit. It's a win-win.

"I came here to say thank you," she says, still pissed at me.

"You're welcome." I pause. "What did I do?"

"You sent my dad season tickets."

"Wait. Briggs? Alexander Briggs was your father?"

She nods.

Damn. She's his daughter? He was my coach when I was in the youth league. I remember he had a kid about a year and a half after I moved to another league. We kept in touch over the years. He always talked about his little girl. I haven't seen him in a few years. The team he coaches reached out to me a little over a year ago, said he had a brain tumor, and asked for tickets to a game for him. I had our ticketing agent send him the season passes that would normally go to my family. He'll keep getting them until I'm traded off or I retire. It was the least I could do for the man who helped turn me into the player I am.

"Is he here?" I ask.

Pain flashes in her gaze, cutting through the chaotic snarl of my mind.

"No," she whispers. "He, um, he died two months ago."

Ah, baby.

As someone who lost both parents early, I know how fucking awful it is. Unless my math is wrong, she's nineteen. Far too goddamn young to be out in the world without someone looking after her. From what I can recall, her mom ran off to London years ago.

"Briggs was a good coach," I say, my voice gruff with sympathy and regret. I should have tried to go see him instead of putting it off. "I imagine he was a hell of a father too. I'm sorry for your loss."

"Thanks. He loved hockey...and you." She rolls her eyes when she says this, which makes me want to chuckle. I don't think she shares her dad's opinion of me.

"What's your seat number?" I ask.

"Why?"

"No reason," I lie.

I don't think she believes me. Her eyes come back to mine, rife with suspicion. She doesn't seem to like me very much. Which isn't surprising since women usually don't like me. But definitely problematic since I actually want this one to like me.

"Can we start over?"

"So you can offer to sign my boobs again? No thanks," she says, her nose wrinkling.

"I can't be blamed for that. Your tits are fucking incredible," I say and then, because I can't help it even though there's a little voice screeching a warning in the back of my head, I add, "Someday, you'll agree to let me sign them."

"You...you...ugh!" Laney growls, throwing her hands up.

See? Honesty definitely is not the best policy.

"I shouldn't have said that."

"You think?" She scowls at me.

Christ, she's a cutie pie. I quickly check her finger to make sure there isn't a ring on it. There isn't, thank God. Which means there's nothing stopping me from making her mine.

Cutie Pie is available now.

Nichole's Book Beauties

Want to connect with Nichole and other readers? We're building a girl gang! Join Nichole Rose's Book Beauties on Facebook for fun, games, and behind-the-scenes exclusives!

Instalove Book Club

The Instalove Book Club is now in session!

Get the inside scoop from your favorite instalove authors, meet new authors to love, and snag a free book and bonus content from featured authors every month. The Instalove Book Club newsletter goes out once per week!

Join the Club: http://instalovebookclub.com

Follow Nichole

Like free books? Me too! Sign-up for my mailing list at http://authornicholerose.com/newsletter to stay up-to-date on all new releases and for exclusive giveaways and freebies!

Want to connect with me and other readers? Join Nichole Rose's Book Beauties on Facebook!

Grab signed copies of books, book boxes, and more at http://nicholerose.shop.

facebook.com/AuthorNicholeRose/

instagram.com/AuthorNicholeRose

twitter.com/AuthNicholeRose

bookbub.com/authors/nichole-rose

tiktok.com/@authornicholerose

Also by Nichole Rose

Find links to my books, audiobooks, the suggested reading order, and a downloadable map of how books connect on my website at http://authornicholerose. com!

Her Alpha Series
Her Alpha Daddy Next Door
Her Alpha Boss Undercover
Her Alpha's Secret Baby
Her Alpha Protector
Her Date with an Alpha
Her Alpha: The Complete Series

Her Bride Series
His Future Bride
His Stolen Bride
His Secret Bride
His Curvy Bride

His Captive Bride
His Blushing Bride
His Bride: The Complete Series

Nashville Lights

Black Velvet
His Secret Obsession
A Hero for Her

Claimed Series

Possessing Liberty
Teaching Rowan
Claiming Caroline
Kissing Kennedy
Claimed: The Complete Series

Love on the Clock Series

Adore You
Hold You
Keep You
Protect You
Love on the Clock: The Complete Series

<u>The Billionaires' Club</u>

The Billionaire's Big Bold Weakness

The Billionaire's Big Bold Wish

The Billionaire's Big Bold Woman

The Billionaire's Big Bold Wonder

The Billionaires' Club: The Complete Series

<u>Playing for Keeps</u>

Cutie Pie

Ice Breaker

Ice Prince

Ice Giant

Cold as Ice

Ice Storm

Playing for Keeps: The Complete Series

<u>Full-Length Titles</u>

Crash into You

Mister Gregory

Fight for You

Kill for You (coming soon)

God of War

The Second Generation
A Blushing Bride for Christmas
Piped Down

Love Bites
Come Undone
Dripping Pearls

Echoes of Forever
His Christmas Miracle
Taken by the Hitman
Wicked Saint

The Ruined Trilogy
Physical Science
Wrecked
Wanton
Wicked
Ruined: The Complete Series

Illicit Love Series
Irresistible

Irrevocable

Irreplaceable

Irredeemable

The Galentines Collection

Romancing the Cowboy

Beach House Beauty

Pretty Little Mess

Hitched to the Heartthrob

Club Dionysus

Dear Mr. Dad Bod

Seduced by Sin (coming soon)

Sinful Obsession (coming soon)

Standalone Titles

A Touch of Summer

Dirty Boy

Naughty Christmas

Naughty Little Elf

Tempted by December

Chasing Christmas

Dear Santa

Easy on Me
Easy Ride
Easy Surrender

One Night with You
Falling Hard
Model Behavior
Learning Curve
Angel Kisses

Carmichael Security Series
Truly Mine
Madly Yours
Deeply Hers

Silver Spoon MC
The Surgeon
The Heir
The Lawyer
The Prodigy

The Bodyguard

Silver Spoon MC Collection: Nichole's Crew

<u>Silver Spoon Falls</u>

Xavier's Kitten

Callum's Hope

Snow's Prince

Aurora's Knight

<u>Silver Spoon Falcons</u>

Leia's Playmaker

Aspen's Defense

Gabbi's Goalie

<u>Silver Spoon After Dark</u>

Bound by Bronx

Coming for Coby

Daddy for Davina

<u>Silver Spoon Connections</u>

Devil's Deceit

<u>writing with Loni Ree as Loni Nichole</u>

Dillon's Heart

Razor's Flame

Ryker's Reward

Zane's Rebel

Oral Arguments

Grizz's Passion

Garrett's Obsession

The Daddy Claus

Submitting to Slade

Dating the Billionaire

Paranormal & Fantasy Titles

A Bride for the Beast (writing with Fern Fraser)

Beauty in Darkness (formerly Beauty's Twisted Tyrant)

Valkyrie Bound

Valkyrie Heart

Valkyrie Fate

Valkyrie Soul

About Nichole Rose

Three-time award-winning author Nichole Rose writes filthy romance for curvy readers. Her books feature headstrong, sassy women and the alpha males who consume them. From obsessed mafia bosses to over-the-top hockey players to ancient Fae warriors and Daddy Doms, nothing is off-limits.

She is sure to have a steamy story just right for everyone. She fully believes the world is ugly enough without trying to fit falling in love into a one-size-fits-all box.

Nichole also writes dark romance as Nichole Fallon.

When not writing, Nichole enjoys fine wine, cute shoes, and everything supernatural. She is happily married to the love of her life and is a proud ringleader in the world's most ridiculous chihuahua circus. She and her husband live in central Arkansas.

You can learn more about Nichole and her books at authornicholerose.com.

facebook.com/AuthorNicholeRose/

instagram.com/AuthorNicholeRose

twitter.com/AuthNicholeRose

bookbub.com/authors/nichole-rose

tiktok.com/@authornicholerose

www.ingramcontent.com/pod-product-compliance
Lightning Source LLC
Chambersburg PA
CBHW070857160726
48004CB00003B/1126